NOT TOO FAR

Southern Hills MRS Series

DANYELLE SCROGGINS

PUBLISHING
WWW.DANYELLESCROGGINS.COM
Email: danyellyourpublishing@gmail.com

"Scripture quotations taken from the New American Standard Bible®, Copyright © 1960, 1962, 1963, 1968, 1971, 1972, 1973, 1975, 1977, 1995 by The Lockman Foundation

Used by permission." (www.Lockman.org)

Published by: Divinely Sown (DS Publishing)

NOT TOO FAR

SOUTHERN HILLS MRS BOOK 1

Previously Published As: NOT TOO FAR GONE

Copyright © 2022 by Danyelle Scroggins

Second Edition paperback

10 9 8 7 6 5 4 3 2 1

Printed in the United States of America

Book Cover Design by Danyelle Scroggins

Exclusive discounts are available for quantity purchases. For details, contact the publisher at the address above.

Printed in the United States of America

Dedicated to

To Educators who love what they do and do it for the children they love.
Thank you!

"Train up a child in the way he should go: and when he is old, he will not depart from it."

Proverbs 22:6

ABOUT NOT TOO FAR

SOUTHERN HILLS MRS BOOK ONE

Is anything ever too far gone, for repair, restoration, or renewal? Never!

Jacqueline Vance might think so, because her world has come crashing down. In her thirties, married, and childless. She becomes the center of a murder mystery in Southern Hills. She learns in the face of the worse betrayal, no one is ever too far gone for God. Not even her coworker and fair-weather friend, Yolanda.

She learns how to fight through what is, to embrace what can be.

Bradley and his daughter Denisia have lost their everything. The glue that held their family together...his wife and her mother. He learns that being a present daddy, has the potential to heal his heart, change his mind, and bring him to his future.

The Southern Hills community learns that failures exist where faith isn't. And that they only presents opportunities for God to display His potential.

Will Jacqueline learn how to fight through what is, to embrace what can be? Will Bradley let go of the past to embrace his future? Or will they falter thinking things are too far gone for even God.

JACQUELINE

"Do you have Shayla Smith in your fifth-hour class?" Jacqueline Vance asked her longtime friend. Jacqueline was a brilliant ten-year math teacher at Yorkwood High School in Shreveport. She was humble with southern reserve and superstar looks which put you in the mind of Beyoncé.e

"I sure do, and that chick is giving me the blues," Yolanda Clark responded. Yolanda was the exact opposite of Jacqueline which made their friendship work. She was not humble at all, and her exotic flare was the first thing you noticed at first glance. Meeting Yolanda put you in the mind of *Nicki* meets *Mariah:* ghetto, glossy, and glamorous and all at the same time.

"Something is happening at home because every day, she comes to my class upset. It's like she wakes up angry and anger follows her throughout the day. Mr. Jacobs sent her to the office yesterday, and I heard the secretary say she cursed them out." Jacqueline inquired with a statement, knowing well Yolanda didn't care either way. She continued on, "They mentioned how she cursed like a fifty-year-old sailor. After-ward she retrieved her purse from the counter and told them she was going to the bathroom. Well, I hear she never came back. Your boss was suspending her for a couple of days. And for some unknown reason, decided to drop the suspension and let her into class today."

"I don't know what Brandon did that for. All he does is sit his fat butt in that office and drink coffee. Then he leaves us to deal with the monsters," Yolanda said, folding her arms and scorching mad.

"Girl," Jacqueline exclaimed with passion, "you can't label them as monsters!"

"Oh yes, I can!" Yolanda answered before finishing her statement. "They don't have any home training at all. These children are too far gone to come back. And no one in administration seems to notice our classrooms are more like circuses."

"Yeah, I guess you're right. I still won't go as far by calling them monsters. There has to be something going on. Do you remember when we were children? Our parents raised us and not our siblings. We had a fear of Jesus and the belt, which kept us grounded." Jacqueline stated, knowing well her dad would still beat her if she got out of line now, and she was grown.

"These days, if you beat their butts, you go to jail," Yolanda stated, rolling her eyes. "Even if you threaten to beat them, they can call the police or social services on you. This is why I will never have children, and furthermore they don't pay us to find out what's going on with these children. They don't even compensate us enough to teach them."

"I can't argue with you about our pay but what I do know is if someone doesn't help her, she will be spending some time in jail." Jacqueline said, shaking her head from side to side.

"Well, you do you at 3:30, when that bell rings, I'm running to my car. I'm going to buy myself a stiff martini, take a bubble bath, get up in my bed, and forget about this school. I'm also forgetting the person who runs this school, and the children who need it but don't realize it." Yolanda responds in her typical couldn't care less dialect. Everyone knew she was only there for the paycheck she complained about. Because of her attitude, no one dared to ask her why she even became an English teacher in the first place.

"Okay girl, I guess I'll connect with you after school or Monday." Jacqueline replied, knowing there was no need to say more. She and

Yolanda were two different persons and personalities. They thought differently as well. She could not expect Yolanda to be as passionate about the children as she was. But she did wish one day she would start to care about them.

"Only, if I don't decide to take one of my sick days," Yolanda said as she turned and went to her class. Jacqueline wanted her to at least act like she cared about these hard-headed children. She wasn't wasting her time. Especially on folks who did not seem to care about themselves. If they did, they would come into the free classrooms, taught by under-paid teachers, and learn.

Jacqueline walked back to her class and closed the door. Complete knowledge of how bad the school system had become over the course of the ten years, stared her in the face. Her mother retired as an educator after thirty-eight years. Seeing all the kids she'd touched made Jacqueline want to follow in her footsteps. Students were not as easy to teach as they were when her mom taught. Things were different and their situations weighed heavy on her heart.

She often thought of changing professions. Each time she decided to leave the school system, something happened to make her stay. Unfortunately, there weren't too many jobs you could be off on weekends and every holiday. The pay did not compensate for all the work rendered, but she'd managed with what she earned. Also, marriage made finances much more manageable.

It was usual for Jacqueline to talk with Yolanda, an English teacher in her thirties like her. They received their master degrees at the same time at LSUS in Shreveport. Fate had it where they taught at the same high school and across the hall from one another. The other differences between them, Yolanda was single and satisfied. Well at least to a point. Yolanda didn't go to church anywhere.

She claimed that she had more education than most of the pastors. She also had no problem voicing how sick and tired she was with them butchering the English language. And preaching for the sake of entertainment. Preachers weren't the only ones on her 'Not-To-Do' list. Yolanda was avid about not wanting to parent children, which was why marriage was on the list.

Every guy who tried to date her had children or wanted children. She didn't have the time to deal with baby mamma drama, and she wasn't going to become a baby mamma with drama. Yolanda knew she was the queen of drama and the first time her child support check was late, she was bound to set it off. So for the world's safety, she decided a safe quickie here or there would suit her fine.

Jacqueline was altogether different. She married a darker skinned curly hair replica of Shamar Moore named Raphiel. Together since they married six years ago, they prayed daily for God to send her a child. But every time she got pregnant, she could not carry to term. They'd gone to every fertility clinic in the city. Spent plenty of money on fertilization shots but still, no baby. After visiting with her pastor, she got confirmation. He convinced her that God had more work for her and Raphiel to do. Now she rested on the fact that when their work was complete, He'd allow them to walk in the purpose of parenting.

It was twenty minutes after two, and she had five minutes before her next math class. She kneeled down at her desk and said a quick prayer...."Lord, please allow this next class to be calm. I pray you'll send angels of peace and quietness to overtake this room right now in the name of Jesus." Then she got up from the prayer position and dusted her knees off.

It had been a long day and after dealing with little Ms. Shayla Smith, she couldn't take any more misbehaving. She wanted to end the school day on the best note possible. Though it seemed hardly unlikely, she knew God could do things humans couldn't. When the bell rang, she opened her door and stood in the hallway to greet her students like normal. As they piled in one by one, she wondered if they knew how essential education was.

Her great-grandmother told her without an education, you might as well be a slave. She showed her the scripture, "My people perish for lack of knowledge." This was the very reason she decided to get all the knowledge she could hold. As the tardy bell rang, she had one or two students running to get in the door before she closed it. Once her door closed, they knew they weren't getting in.

"Good afternoon, students," Jacqueline smirked as she thought about what Yolanda calls them.

"Hey, Mrs. Vance," they yelled back.

"Before we get started, can anyone tell me what we talked about yesterday?" she asked, hoping someone could answer and at the same time reassure her that teaching was not in vain.

Some of the students raised their hands as others began to yell out the answer.

"We talked about the importance of the dollar. You also said how our currency can multiply over time in the right money markets," Sherell Jones said. She sounded confident and assured as she overpowered everyone else's response.

"You are right, Ms. Jones. Now today, we are going to be taking a look at saving bonds, the different IRAs, and CDs."

"I have a couple of savings bonds I can't cash until I'm eighteen," Eric Mitchell said.

"Yeah, we know you, the rich boy. You better shut up before I jack you."

"All right, Clarence!" Jacqueline spoke firm and aggressive. She turned her body in the direction of the sixteen year old who portrays himself as a gangster. "You will not be jacking anyone up in here or on the streets. If I ever hear of you jacking anybody, I'm going to jack you," Jacqueline points right at him with no fear in her heart.

"Ahh, Mrs. Vance, you know I was playing," Clarence said with a huge smile plastered on his lips.

"Well, Mr. Clarence, we don't play like that?"

"We don't play like thugs," he replied, knowing that was how she felt and her very next response.

"You think you know me well, now let's move on. First, did everyone bring their decorated jar for the savings plan? If you did, you would get extra credit." Jacqueline's heart melted because everyone except Clarence had brought their jar. She kind of figured that he wouldn't so she made him give her two dollars so she could buy his.

"Clarence, here is your jar. Go put it back there with the others. Now, did everyone bring the dollar for their jar?"

"Yes," the teens replied in unison.

"Well, put it in your jars and remember to bring your dollar a day for the next thirty days."

"Okay," they responded. She, with enthusiasm, began to teach the class.

She explained the differences in IRAs. When most of the students understood, she moved to savings bonds. Everyone seemed to be appreciating the class, and she was sure her prayer had worked. None of them were loud or disrespectful, and she was actually enjoying her class. She looked up at her clock. It was five minutes until the ringing of the bell and was ecstatic that her students wanted her to keep going. She didn't know if the peaking of their interest came by what she was teaching. Or it could have been the fact that their money could grow by sitting. Either way she was happy.

Jacqueline learned at an early age the value of saving money. Her parents also taught principles for preparing for financial stability. But most of her students weren't taught how to do anything with money but how to spend, hustle for, or beg for it. They seemed to come to school with plenty of money with no plans on how to spend or save it. Eric Mitchell, whose mother was a supervisor at the local bank, was the only one who had any money saved. Math was often a sore subject for students. As much as they feared math, she feared they would never know the value of money.

Jacqueline figured what better way to teach math than teaching about money. Most of the kids she taught would never apply math after high school to anything except money. She supposed if they didn't go to college, preparing them about money for their future might help.

When the bell rang, she packed her briefcase. Then she put the children's jars in a locked safety box she'd purchased for the project, and turned off her lights. She was leaving out the door when she turned around as if she forgot something.

"Lord, I want to thank you for sending your angels to do the job. Now, if it's not too much to ask, would you please let these same angels meet me here on Monday. I need them like I need my job; in Jesus's name. Amen."

She left the room, closing the door, and making sure it was locked. She looked over at Yolanda's classroom which was dark. She figured she was already gone. She couldn't help but praise the Lord for the weekend. It had been a long week, and she was in need of rest.

She didn't get too far down the hall before she heard her name. "Hey, Mrs. Vance," the voice coming from behind her spoke as loud as her children. "I heard you had a round today with Ms. Smith." Mr. Marvin Jacobs yells from three doors down. He was an African American Pee Wee Herman look-alike who taught history.

"Mr. Jacobs, I don't know what's going on with that child. On my break, I tried calling her mother, but I didn't get an answer."

"Vance, I don't even call homes anymore. When I did call their homes, the children got worse. I don't know what to say about young people these days." Mr. Jacobs exclaimed.

"Well, the Bible says they'll grow weaker and wiser, and I do believe it's coming to pass. It sickens me to even think about them taking prayer out of schools. Mr. Jacobs, these children need Jesus and all the prayer they can get," Jacqueline replied.

"I know, and that's exactly why I bring my Bible to school every day. Between classes if I didn't get some Word in me, I'd strangle one of them or myself," Mr. Jacobs starts laughing.

"Well, I pray you do neither so keep on reading that Word." Jacqueline, who was as tickled as him, shook one of her hands in the air. "I hope you enjoy your weekend because I sure do plan on enjoying mine."

"Me too, and thank you," Mr. Jacobs replied.

After her unwanted conversation, she almost ran to her car in hopes that no one else would call her name. Jacqueline loved all things about teaching. She couldn't stand teachers who always pointed out the student's problems. Those who never tried to figure out the root causes of the problem. Jacqueline jumped in and started her car. Before she put the car in gear, she put in the smooth listening tunes of Jill Scott. There was something jazzy and majestic in her voice. *This girl could calm a raging sea.*

As she nodded her head to the soulful beats, she put her car in reverse. Jacqueline looked up into her rearview mirror to make sure the way was clear. She noticed a young man snatching a girl who she couldn't quite make out. He was talking loud, but she couldn't make out what he was saying above the music.

Deciding to take the long way out of the parking lot to get a better look, she drove slow. In her heart, she determined this situation was worth being nosey. As soon as they noticed her car approaching, the girl jumped in the car, and they sped off. Jacqueline couldn't help wondering if this was child abduction. Had the girl been snatched against her will? The fact she wasn't screaming made her come to the swift conclusion -- it was a teenage lover's quarrel.

She turned her attention back to her groove and sang the words to "Golden." She'd had enough of Yorkwood High to last her until Monday morning. Then her mind switched to a more personal situation. She put her foot on the accelerator and pushed the remote to let the top back in her car. She wished going home meant going to find a man who loved, watched, and waited for her to come through the doors.

Wishful thinking I guess, but a girl does have the right to dream doesn't she?

THE GANGSTA & SHAYLA

"I tell you what; you have two seconds to get your butt in this car."

"I don't want to go with you!"

"Girl, you think I came all the way down here so your ratchet tail could tell me what you wanted. Your crackhead momma didn't pay me for my stuff, and I am going to get paid one way or the other."

"Please, let me go home."

"You can go anywhere you want to go when I get through with you."

YOLANDA

Yolanda decided since she had parked in the back of the school, she might as well leave. No one could see her anyway. She'd been at York-wood long enough for one day, and a stiff margarita was calling her name. She drove to Tequila Delights and a trip that should have taken her fifteen minutes only took five. She pulled her wallet out of her purse and the keys out of the ignition; with one thing on her mind… her happy land.

"Hi there, Ms. Yolanda, you're early today. Will it be your regular?" Michelle, the cashier at Tequila Delights, asked. She smiled as soon as she saw Yolanda. It tickled her to see the interaction between Yolanda and her boss Bradley Johnson. Bradley always hit on her, knowing all too well that if she had agreed to his advances, he would have fallen flat out. Yolanda was not the type of woman he wanted with Denisia, his three-year-old daughter. Michelle knew that as a matter of fact.

"Yes, love, and put an extra shot in there for me. Those kids drove me nuts, and when I get home, I'm going to drink and relax." Yolanda started rolling her eyes and moving her head up and down to a beat in her own head.

"I sure wish I could go home with you," Bradley Johnson said, coming from the back of the store. Bradley was a tall, caramel colored man who always dressed to impress. Any woman might consider having this wonderful specimen of a man on their arms, but not Yolanda Clark.

"Baby, you can't afford me. And you know I don't fool with nobody's daddy." Yolanda answered with her eyes bucked and a sneaky and wicked smile.

"Yeah, you've told me over and over again," Bradley answered with a slight laugh of his own.

"So when will you get the picture, baby?" Yolanda said.

Leaving Bradley no choice but to voice his actual opinion. "You women always talk about wanting a good man. When a good man is standing right in front of you, you are too darn crazy to know it."

"Say what you want. All you can do for me is fix my drinks as I pay you to," Yolanda answered, feeling no remorse, guilt, or shame.

"Yes, ma'am," Bradley answered while touching Michelle, who was laughing the whole time. He was a God-fearing man, and even though he owned a liquor store, he was picky about women.

"Don't go trying to make me feel old as dust," Yolanda shouted.

"Well, that is exactly what you're going to be when you find a man that doesn't have kids. If a man is over thirty-five without a wife or child, it's a good chance the brother is gay." Bradley stated as if he wrote the statistics himself.

"That's what you say. If it goes that way, then that's how your God meant it to be," Yolanda said. Bradley Johnson believed everything there was to believe about God. He had long stated claims on God in her presence.

"The drinks are on the house today, lady," he said, handing her the plastic Styrofoam cup. The lid covered with a strip of tape on top of the straw hole was the legal way of protecting the customers. Drinking and driving was never cool.

"Thanks, Brad, I guess I'll see you when I want another one," Yolanda said as she walked out of Tequila Delights.

Yolanda knew Bradley would date her if he had half the chance, what man wouldn't? She'd had a couple of heated conversations with him before he got saved, married, and had a baby. Now that he was a single parent, she didn't have anything for him; not even a conversation outside of his business.

Although his baby momma could give her no drama where she was, she still didn't want the responsibility. Yet again another thing on her list. No fooling with anyone's child after hours. After she left Yorkwood High, there wasn't any room in her life for a child.

A stiff drink and a stiff "one" was all she had room for. When the drink was gone, in the trash the cup went, and when she finished with the man, out her door he'd go. Yolanda peered at the cup that seemed to be calling her name. She could hardly wait to make it home to put her straw in the Styrofoam cup. She'd waited all day with flashes of her favorite drink on her tongue. Yet being the moral citizen she was, she refused to drink and drive. When she finally made it home, she realized if she were more relaxed, her drink would taste even better.

As soon as she unlocked her door, she put her stuff on the coffee table. Yolanda strolled into the kitchen and placed her drink in the freezer. Her game plan was set. Straight to the tub, take a bath, and relax. She added some watermelon scented soap to the water. Then she lit two watermelon scented candles and placed them on the corners of the tub. "Yes," she said, inhaling the scent. Yolanda opened the Pandora app and requested the Maze Station. When the mood was set, she pulled off her clothes and got in the tub.

She started singing, "We Are One" by Maze, but had no intentions of ever being one with anyone. She was the stereotypical female who claimed to be single and satisfied, but was the first and not the last. A woman controlled by her come and go longing to have a man and when the need hit, accepted anything. With Yolanda, either you had what she wanted, or you didn't. Until she found it, she was going to use the ones she could get pleasure out of. *Happy and satisfied.*

After her bubble bath, she slipped into a little pink teddy with the matching robe. She strolled to the kitchen as if she were on a Paris runway to retrieve her drink. After she took a sip and made a sound which indicated it was how she liked it, she went back to her bedroom. It was time to get in the center of her bed, and turn on the television. After flipping the channels for a while, she found an excellent jazz show to watch. Thirty minutes later after the commercial went off, she heard, "If you aren't saved, now is the time to give God your hand."

"What happened to the jazz show?" She picked up the remote to make sure she hadn't changed the channel. "Y'all are always messing stuff up with this dollar grabbing, lying Prophet, who only wants folk's money."

Then she decided to turn the television off. She'd had a long day, and wasn't going to end it with some creep telling her she needed salvation. Then asking her for money. She'd had all she could take with these preachers. Yolanda hadn't known one preacher who was real. All the ones she ever came in contact with wanted money or a cootie cat. The name her mother gave a woman's vagina that stuck with for life.

If they started out right in the beginning and she kept going long enough, they'd find a way to ask her for what was hers. Although she didn't mind giving it up, she wasn't privy to giving nothing to someone who claimed they belonged to God. She didn't need their fat behinds having a heart attack on top or under her. She'd come to a conclusion long ago the church had nothing to offer her except a collection plate and a bogus man.

Yolanda sipped her drink and turned her thoughts to the flavor of the night. Tonight's dish of delight was a man she referred to as "mister do me right." He could please her in ways she'd never imagined, but that wasn't enough for her.

Nonetheless, the extra big head hundreds he dropped every time he visited made him worth it. Although he almost fit the criteria she wanted, he was a church boy and she wasn't going to anybody's church. He was all good until he started talking about Jesus and prayer meeting discussions. She ushered him to the door, using whatever excuse she could to confirm that it was time for him to leave. She noticed the time, and decided it was time to move. Yolanda got out of the bed, fixed her hair, and put a little makeup on. She needed to be cute when he arrived and her aim was to burst his heart and his head. While she waited, she decided to call to check on her co-worker.

Ring. Ring. Ring.

BRADLEY

Bradley Johnson was the sole owner of Tequila Delights. He didn't enjoy the business like he did when he started it, but then he was a drinker. He'd come into some money when his grandfather died and decided to buy a business he would enjoy as much as his buddies. Now, his buddies were still enjoying the benefits of a homeboy with a liquor store. But he no longer enjoyed being the one who supplied everyone with their liquor. There was a time in his life when nothing much mattered; but after losing his wife in a car accident, things changed.

Now he was a single parent raising his three-year-old daughter Denisia. Bradley tried hard to be as responsible of a father as he could be. His dad wasn't there for him, and now he had no choice but be there for his little girl. Without an example of a man within his bloodline, he had to depend on prayer.

He was ready to have a woman in his life to love him and help him take care of Denisia, but any woman wouldn't do. He often played around with the women he knew wouldn't give him the time of day, and he did it because he knew it. The woman who came into his life would not drink alcohol. She also had to love kids, which made Yolanda Clark a complete no.

Bradley closed the store drive-thru window, and then double

checked to make sure it was locked. He was happy about it being time to go home. It was ten o'clock and he'd been at the liquor store since nine in the morning.

As he locked the store he thanked God. He knew the blessing of having a sweet babysitter who didn't mind keeping Denisia as late as he needed her too. Mrs. Burch was an older church mother in her late sixties who owned two daycares. After the death of his wife, she'd done whatever she could to make life easier for him and his daughter. And now, she was like a second mother to him and grandmother to Denisia. As soon as he pulled up in her driveway, the porch light came on and the front door opened.

"Hey, darling, how was your night?" Mrs. Burch asked Bradley as she unlocked the screen door.

"Mother Burch, it was long," he answered, reaching in to hug her as soon as she swung the screen door open.

"Well, you have to do what you have to do. That little angel of yours is in the guest bedroom. She was good as usual but for some reason, today she asked a lot of questions," Mother Burch mentioned.

"I hope she didn't bother you," Bradley said with a look of remorse in his eyes.

"Oh, never," Mrs. Burch replied then finished by saying, "She is the sweetest child I know. Although we both wonder if she'll ever get another mommy. You know children talk and at the daycare, mommies are important."

"I understand. I don't seem to have time to date," Bradley answered. knowing all too well how persistent Denisia could be when she wanted an answer.

"I know," Ms. Burch replied. "You are always working and that's the problem."

"Yes, ma'am, and I don't want to rush it. You know I'm all Dennie has and if I get tied up with the wrong woman, it'll hurt her more than me." Bradley called his baby girl by her nickname.

"I know, baby. Pray and God will send you a woman fit to be your wife."

Bradley wanted to show her that he listened to her. He said, "If you're praying about it, He will." And they both laughed.

If Mrs. Burch wasn't anything else, she was a praying woman who believed in prayer and the power of God. She didn't mind testifying about how God answered all her prayers. It wasn't a boast but rather her trying to convince you to pray.

"Mother Burch, thank you so much. I'm going to get this little one home and in her own bed."

"That's great, and she's already in her nightgown and I'll see you all tomorrow."

"Yes, ma'am," Bradley answered as he put Denisia in the back seat and covered her with her little blanket. She was growing and he was missing out on everything.

Now that Denisia was three, she was a book of questions. Although he never minded answering them, they seemed to have gotten harder. After he laid her down, he kissed her good night, covered her up, and then he went to shower and wind down. After he ate a late night snack and drank a hot cup of tea, usually he watched a little television. But tonight he was too tired to even think about watching TV. The TV would be watching him even if he tried. Instead, he opted to call it a night.

YOLANDA & JACQUELINE

Jacqueline fumbled through her purse until she found her phone. "Hey, lady," she answered on the third ring.

"Hey Jacqueline, what are you doing?"

"Girl, I was about to get in the tub."

Jacqueline finally made it home after stopping by Cooksure's Grocery store. She had a little alone time which proved bitter sweet. She would rather have her husband, Raphiel at home with her. But he was going to Valley High's rival football game against Eagle Christian. Yet, she thought he'd appreciate having dinner waiting whether he ate it or not. He'd been coming in late for the past month. His excuse stemmed around him not being able to get his employees to do anything he asked them.

She rarely complained because she knew how hard he worked to build his company. They both sacrificed so much effort for his vision. Jacqueline worked while she helped Raphiel finish school. And as soon as he finished he decided he wanted a car lot. It only took them six months to plan, and within a year, he'd opened his own car lot. She also seldom visited the car lot because there weren't many women there. Besides Aunt Geraldine, who was Raphiel's aunt, there weren't any women there.

"I've already done all that," Yolanda gloated.

"Who is the flavor for the night?" Jacqueline asked, hearing sneakiness all over Yolanda's tone. She unpacked the groceries. She decided to cook some chicken tacos since they were easy and wouldn't add to her exhaustion. After her quick meal, she put foil over her food and went to run some bath water. She laughed, walking up stairs thinking about Yolanda and what she said she was going to do when she got home.

"What makes you think there is one?" Yolanda asked.

"Yolanda, I know you and if I remember, tonight is," she made air quotes with her fingers, "Mister Do You Right time?"

"Jacqueline, you think you know me."

"We've only been friends for twelve years or better."

"Whatever," Yolanda said. "We are only 'work friends' because we never hang out after work or go anywhere together. Isn't it strange that I've never met your husband?"

Jacqueline laughed. "No, because you never have time and I don't need a single woman hanging around my man. Better yet, I don't know why you keep selling yourself short. These guys aren't worth it and you are too old for all this man swapping." Jacqueline preached. She knew that it was going straight out of her mouth and through Yolanda's ears.

Jacqueline knew she and Yolanda had hardly anything in common except being teachers. Jacqueline couldn't imagine sleeping around with so many men and Yolanda had made a hobby out of it. She had always heard opposites attract and in their case, they couldn't have been any more opposite. Jacqueline knew one thing for sure about Yolanda; if you were her friend she loved you.

The other thing she knew all too well was Yolanda wanted to hear nothing about Jesus. She admitted believing in God. But her reasoning for staying away from Christians was the dirt they did. She couldn't understand folks who go around claiming to be a Christian but did dirt every chance they got. Jacqueline tried hard to explain that we all are sinners saved by grace. But Yolanda's argument was why do I need the classification of a Christian when I'm going to sin. A lot of times Jacqueline felt like she had a good argument. They were good enough but not good enough for her not to believe or embrace the title of a Christian.

"Okay then, I guess you're alright," Yolanda said, aiming to stop the preaching before it began. "I'm hurt that you think I'd mess with your man though. I do have a heart, Jacqueline."

They'd been friends for quite some time, but rarely did anything together outside of school. It wasn't because Jacqueline didn't invite her. Yolanda always said they were friends traveling in different circles. She wouldn't get caught dead in the places Jacqueline went, and Jacqueline felt the same way. There was no way you'd catch her in a club or even a liquor store.

When she was saved, her plan was to stay saved. And anything that would make her do something not in God's will as alcohol did, she didn't want any parts of it. She'd even tried inviting Yolanda to her home, but Yolanda said it wouldn't be right because she wasn't invited to hers. Jacqueline could have taken offense. But she could only imagine what was going down in Yolanda's house, and wanted no parts of it either. She often asked herself the question about their relationship. Like how can two walk together except they agree? Jacqueline figured God would show her why she got connected to Yolanda.

"I know you wouldn't do anything to hurt me and stop trying to blow me off. I don't know what I'm going to do with you," Jacqueline said.

"Love me," Yolanda said. "Okay, girl, I'll be talking with you."

"Goodnight and make him wear a condom," Jacqueline screams. Yolanda laughed as she hung up without responding.

All in all, Yolanda made Jacqueline aware of one thing, your home life is your home life. No one had any business knowing what went on. Unlike a lot of teachers, Jacqueline found it unnecessary to have Raphiel at her job. She didn't even share pictures of their life. Home and job were separate and she'd planned on keeping it that way.

She loved her home, but at times the house was tranquil. Lately, the silence was beginning to get to Jacqueline. Getting the remedy to her dilemma, she went to the sound system and turned it on. She'd been playing the *Rebirth of Kirk Franklin* on Sunday morning, and it was still in the CD player. She didn't bother to change it because Kirk had a way of making her think about someone other than herself, Jesus. And as anointed as he was, she thought he was the funniest gospel artist around. She even began to smile thinking of him yelling, "Jimmy," on *Sunday's Best*, a television gospel show which he hosted.

She finally drifted off to sleep.

Jacqueline got up to go to the bathroom and realized Raphiel wasn't home. It was becoming frequent to have him out until the next morning at least once a week. She hadn't been too bothered by it because he always hung out at the pubs with his friends from work. She hadn't expected him to hang out so long or frequently.

She washed her hands, looked at her face in the mirror, and went back to bed. It wasn't like Raphiel didn't care, because every time he'd stayed out late he apologized for it. Then he promised to be cautious the next time. Somehow his staying out was becoming a bit easier for him after every episode. She didn't want to ever come across as the over-bearing wife, so she accepted his excuses. As Jacqueline laid in bed looking at the ceiling, an uneasy feeling hit her. As the time kept moving, the more uneasy she felt. She decided to pray for her husband.

"Lord, please watch over Raphiel. I don't know what's going on with him but I know you know. Lord, I know if you keep him, he's kept. I love you Lord and I thank you, in Jesus's name. Amen."

Prayer always brought peace to her mind whenever something bothered or upset her. It had been her absolute safety umbrella through many things. After she prayed she turned over in a fetal position and finally drifted back to sleep.

THE GANGSTA & SHAYLA

"Go in there and get your lazy, addicted momma and get the hell out of my house."

She put her hands on her hips, "How are we supposed to get home?"

"I don't give a ---- how you get there. I want both of you out of my house now."

"Come on Momma. You have to wake up. Come on."

He played with the gun in his hands. "You got thirty minutes to get her out of here, and you better be gone when I get back, or it will be hell to pay."

She rolled her eyes. "Okay."

"I know you aren't talking sharp to me." He said snatching her head in his hands, almost throwing her head into the small of her back.

"I'm not getting smart, we'll be gone."

"You better." And he got his keys and left.

Lord, if you don't see me as people do, please get us out of here. Please wake her up so we can go. Lord, if you never do anything else for me, please do this for me. If you are real, Jesus, I am praying in your name because that preacher said if we do it in your name you hear it.

"Baby, is that you?" The woman half dazed, half awake asked.

"Come on momma. Get up so we can get out of here!"

Like a child who had no clue where they were, she asked, "Where are we at baby?"

"Momma, don't worry, come on."

She called the taxi company's dispatcher. "Could you send a taxi to 3228 Malcolm Street and please hurry?"

"One is on the way. Will someone be standing out or will he need to blow?"

"Please don't let them blow. We'll be waiting outside for him."

"Come on momma, let's go outside. Hold on to me and walk fast."

"Okay baby."

About ten minutes later the cab driver pulled up in front of them. She put her mother into the cab and then climbed in behind her. "Sir, drive us to the shelter on Fern and Texas."

"I will. Now, do you have enough fare to pay for the ride?"

"Yeah, I wouldn't have called you if I didn't. Now stop asking me questions and take us where I told you to take us."

RAPHIEL

Raphiel was a chocolate man with a body that made you think of an NFL superstar. Most women thought he was attractive, even his wife Jacqueline, but he didn't buy into his looks. Looks could do nothing for his pockets and at this point in his life, his pockets were his greatest concern.

He looked over at the clock and noticed time had slipped by. He jumped up and put on his tailor-made Steve Harvey suit, and then grabbed his keys. He wondered what on earth Jacqueline was going to say. This was the fourth night he didn't make it home until the next morning. It was two o'clock in the morning and he hadn't seen his home or his wife since eight o'clock the previous morning.

Raphiel unlocked the front door and walked into the house. He made sure the door didn't make any noise so he would not awake Jacqueline. Then he tiptoed up the stairs and peeked into their bedroom door at his wife who lay asleep. He closed the door and went to the downstairs bathroom to shower. It was obvious by how tired he was that his tail was way too old to be keeping these late night hours. The enjoyment made time not a factor.

He suspected Jacqueline knew he wasn't home so he decided early on not to lie. He would explain to her how time had slipped away but this time, unlike the others, he wasn't going to apologize. Why should he apologize for having the time of his life? He was his own man and he didn't have to apologize for being a man.

Raphiel managed to escape Jacqueline's presence again. Although he didn't apologize, at least he did leave her a nice little note and some breakfast on the stove, he thought. That was the least he could do for her because he did love Jacqueline. He wasn't happy about her inability to have children. He was beginning to think she didn't want to have his child.

Sure they'd gone to all the fertility centers together. It seemed to him Jacqueline wasn't trying hard enough. "If she got pregnant, I'd be a better husband," he thought aloud as he within himself tried to justify his actions.

He didn't have time to keep dwelling on her and the baby he didn't have. He had people all over the car lot looking for every car printed in his sales ad. It was days like today that he enjoyed his job even more than others. If the ad could get him at least forty visitors, he was bound to have at least eighteen cars sold and that was good.

THE GANGSTA & SHAYLA

"I thought I told you to be at my house this morning."

"No, you told me to get my mother and get out and that's what I did."

"Girl, if it weren't for those snooping folks at that schoolhouse I'd have slapped you upside your head. You can say what you want but if you don't come to clean my house today, you'll find your momma in a ditch somewhere."

"How am I going to get there?"

"I don't care how you get here. You better find a way and when you get here, it better look like I have a top-notch cleaning crew."

"Okay, I'm on my way."

JACQUELINE

It was eight in the morning when Jacqueline realized Raphiel never made it to bed. She didn't want to panic so she went to the bathroom and decided to do her morning ritual...pray and then wash her face. After she finished, she put on her robe and slippers and went downstairs to the kitchen. Raphiel had left her some breakfast on the stove with a note that read...

Hey Darling,
I had to be at the office early this morning. Hope you enjoy your breakfast.
Love Raphiel

Jacqueline balled up the note and threw it in the trash. If she wasn't so hungry, she would have thrown the food and the plate in the trash as well. She wasn't going to allow him to ruin her day. She ate her food and after she finished, she decided she would enjoy the rest of her day.

On Saturdays, she did whatever she wanted to do anyway. It was Raphiel's busiest work day and they rarely did anything together on Saturdays. She'd wanted to catch a movie that was receiving rave reviews since its opening day. Jacqueline decided to make it first on her agenda.

Jacqueline pulled her hair up into a ponytail and put on a sweatshirt, some jeans, and a pair of tennis shoes. She wore dress clothes all week and on Saturday she wanted to be the pretty tomboy. Her long pointed nose and high cheekbones were features she'd inherited from her great grandmother. She was as proud of her Indian facial features as she was of her accomplishments. After she put on a little lipstick, she changed purses and headed for the door.

YOLANDA

Yolanda hadn't been awake when her Mister Do You Right left. He'd done the normal; left her sleepy and satisfied like usual. When she woke up, she'd noticed he was in a hurry because he'd left her front door unlocked. Didn't he know someone could have hurt her in the middle of the night? She made a mental note to tell him off as soon as she saw him again.

They didn't get together much because whenever they did, she'd had enough of him to last her for some months. She grabbed an apple out of the refrigerator and went back to bed. All she planned on doing today was recovering from the rendezvous. Getting some much-needed rest was on her agenda as well.

"Oh, I'm such a lucky girl!" she screamed as she kicked her legs up and down on her bed. "Not only did I get laid, I got paid!" she exclaimed as she threw up the ten one hundred dollar bills she discovered under her pillow. She was not in her mind a prostitute or a whoremonger; she was only getting what her goodies were worth. Her daddy told her when she was sixteen, any woman giving up her cookie should never be broke. She held that close to her heart and was sticking to it like it was a rule.

Yolanda watched some old television shows when she finally woke up. She was doing herself a favor by staying in bed all day. When her stomach began to growl, it reminded her she'd only eaten an apple. She went into the bathroom, and ran herself some bath water, deciding to do a lunch run when she finished. As she was about to step into the tub, her doorbell rang.

"Now who could this be?" she questioned herself as she put on the pink robe that hung on the bathroom door at all times.

"Who is it?" she yelled as she came closer to the door.

"Open the door, baby," the familiar voice said and sent chills up and down her spine. It was Mister Do You Right and she was happy he came, even though it was an unannounced visit.

"Hey, darling, I thought you might need a little food."

"I was getting ready to take a bath so I could go get something to eat. Baby, I sure do appreciate this. Now I won't have to leave the house."

"I'll do anything for you, sweet darling. Give me a kiss so I can go." And she planted a huge kiss on his lips.

No other man made her feel the way he did and she was beginning to want his company often. Yolanda wanted to ask him if he could stay a little while longer. She decided against it because she did not want to seem needy. She was an independent woman who did things her own way. She never let a man believe she was head over heels for him, and she wasn't about to start it now.

He was her choice of a lifetime mate but she wasn't sure if she was ready for that or not. The only example of a happy marriage she knew was her friend's. Jacqueline raved about marriage as extended happiness. She swore her marriage made her feel like she had someone in whom she could depend on.

Yolanda didn't doubt Jacqueline's feelings but rarely had she seen a working marriage. All the married people she knew were either divorced or getting ready to go through a divorce. She figured why she would set herself up for a complete letdown. It was easier to sleep with them, get her needs met, and then let them go wherever they went. She rarely even bothered to know anything about them.

Yolanda would never forget the day she met Mr. Do Her Right. She was in the club having a drink and in walked this well dressed distinctive gentleman. The suit he wore was top of the line and his shoes matched his tie and belt to perfection.

As soon as he glazed the room, it didn't take long for their eyes to meet. Before the end of the night, they were at her place in the bed and she didn't even know his name. His friends addressed him as "L," and she referenced him, wonderful. After three nights together, she was becoming attached and for some reason, she wanted to know him.

BRADLEY

Bradley woke up and got dressed. Once he finished grooming himself, he woke up his little angel so she could eat. Denisia hated waking up in the mornings and he almost hated waking her up. She looked so much like her mother when she slept until it was almost unreal. His heart still longed for her and there was nothing he could do about it. As he stood in his daughter's bedroom door glaring down at her, he remembered.

"Mr. Johnson, there's been an accident on 3132 and your wife is here at Louisiana Day Hospital. Is there any way you can come to the 3rd floor?"

"Yes, I'll be there," he said as he hung up the phone.

Nothing in the world would prepare him for what he was about to see. There was his wife, Denise, the love of his life, on a bed with tubes coming and going from all sorts of places. As he held her hand, he cried because he felt deep down she was gone.

"Hi Mr. Johnson, my name is Dr. Razpa and the reason your wife is in my care is because she's six months pregnant. Did you know that she was pregnant?"

Bradley took a moment to answer the doctor because of the lump in his throat. He wanted to break down and fight. *But who?* They'd been trying for years to have a baby and now she was pregnant but would never know the joy of being a mother.

"No, doc, we didn't know she was pregnant."

"Well, she still is. Even though she's unconscious, the baby is fine."

"Why are all the tubes in her?"

"Unfortunately, Mrs. Johnson is not breathing on her own. For the sake of the unborn child, we have her hooked up to breathing monitors so the baby will receive what it needs."

"Are you telling me that Denise is dead, Doctor?"

"I'm sorry to inform you, Mr. Johnson, your wife transpired." Those were the last words he heard before he fell to his knees and everything went black. When he finally woke up, he looked at his parents who seemed to have aged in moments. Worry lines were on their faces and he knew it wasn't a dream. He looked around and saw Denise's parents, Pastor Roderick Strong, and his wife, Destiny.

"How are you, Bradley?" Pastor Strong asked.

"Pastor, I don't know. What happened to me?"

"The nurse said that you passed out and they brought you to this room to recover."

"Denise! Pastor, Denise is gone."

"We know, Bradley. It's such an unfortunate loss, but you know God doesn't make mistakes."

Bradley had always thought that too but taking his wife must've been a mistake. Nothing and no one could have ever prepared him to be without his wife. Now, not only was she gone, but he got left behind alone to raise a child.

"Pastor." And before he could say anything, tears flooded his eyes and pain flooded his heart.

"We know you are hurting, but we also know God is a sovereign God. Denise has finished her work on Earth and it's time for her to go to the place God has prepared for her. We cannot be selfish, Bradley. God blessed her to be with us for some time now and He was gracious enough to spare the life of your child."

"Yes, Bradley, she has been a good daughter to us and a good wife to you. She's taken care of other folks all her life and now it is time for her to rest," Dr. Dennis Hayes, Denise's father, said.

"Why He didn't take me? The baby needs her. I don't know how I'm going to make it without her."

"Bradley, you know how I felt about my grandmother. She was all I had and when she died I felt a hole in my heart, but God. God will keep you in perfect peace if you keep your mind stayed on Him. Don't think about what you're going to need or not need; think about what Denise has now and that is sweet rest. Be happy for her and God will show you that you can make it," First Lady Destiny said and she patted him on the shoulder.

It was no secret how she loved her grandmother who'd raised her after her mother went into the service. Everyone knew Destiny would fall apart when her grandmother died but she didn't. She stayed true to the faith and believed God's word and now she was as happy as ever. Now there he was peering down at the only thing he had left of Denise besides memories.

Denisia was an exact replica of her mother. She had her mother's slanted hazel brown eyes, her long sandy brown hair, and her majestic facial features. It didn't matter what time of day or night, Denise always looked like a complete front cover girl. And so did the little girl she'd left behind. God took his most beloved but had given him a part of her that healed his heart.

Bradley took from her closet Denisia's pink sweatsuit. He found the shoe box labeled pink tennis shoes and pulled it from the top of the closet. Girls had so much stuff and he did not realize it until Denisia came. He found out that boxing and labeling her things made his life easier. So he made sure all her shoes were in plastic labeled containers at the top of her closet.

He went to her hair box and took out some pink bows. Thank God Mrs. Burch always had her hair combed. All he had to do was change the color of her bows to match her clothing, and that was easy. After he had all her things laid out, he woke her and carried her to the bathroom to brush her teeth and wash her face.

"Daddy, are we getting ready to go on our date today?"

"Yes, baby, today is date day and I'm taking you to see a movie."

"Okay, Daddy."

Bradley always wanted Denisia to know she was his main girl. He heard the Pastor say, 'Dads ought to take their daughters on dates so they could see how a young man should treat them.' He took his pastor's advice. Not only did he take her on dates, but he also made sure he gave her flowers and opened doors for her.

Today's flowers were six pink roses. Bradley only gave her six because he felt he could save something for her future husband. If he had it his way, she'd skip dating and marriage altogether.

JACQUELINE

Jacqueline drove up to the theater's preview boards. After surveying everything showing, she realized she'd seen all but three of the movies. She was such a movie-head; one of the things that drew her to Raphiel. Lately, going to the movies has become her only outlet. Raphiel never had time to do anything except work. As much as she hated going by herself, she refused to miss out on the good things of life because of his work schedule.

Going to the movies was one of her favorite activities before she got saved. So, it didn't bother her at all that she'd lose the club gigs. She figured she still came out on top because she could go to the movies and remain saved. The only movies she hadn't seen yet were two horror films and an animated cartoon. She wasn't into horror movies so she figured she'd catch the animated film. If nothing else she was bound to get a much-needed laugh.

She arrived thirty minutes before the show would start, and made perfect use of the extra time. Jacqueline jumped in the popcorn line and purchased some popcorn and a soda. After the cashier handed her the snacks, she adjusted her tote bag on her shoulder.

She needed to finish grading some tests so she figured she would make good use of the extra time. The young attendant saw she had a load and volunteered to help her to her seat. He carried her tote bag and popcorn and she toted her soda and box of candy. She couldn't believe one box of candy cost her two dollars but what the heck, it was her money.

"Ms., this is your movie screen right here at door B."

"Thank you, young man."

"I'll walk you to your seat. Is there anywhere, in particular, you'd like to sit?"

"Why don't you follow me and I'll show you," Jacqueline said. She led the young man up the stairs to a row of seats three rows from the top. She liked sitting up high in order not to feel so close to the screen.

"Thank you, sweetheart. You've been a true gentleman."

"You are welcome, Mrs. Vance."

"You must attend Yorkwood High?"

"Yes, ma'am, I will actually have your class next semester and I'm looking forward to the savings plan," the young man said.

"What is your name?"

"My name is Reginald Steward."

"It was a pleasure to meet you, Mr. Steward, and I'll be looking forward to seeing you in my class."

"Thanks. I better get back to my post, someone else might need help."

"Okay, darling. Have a blessed day now."

"Thanks!" Reginald said before hopping down the stairs by twos.

Right after Jacqueline took her seat, her cell phone rang. She laid her papers in the seat next to her and fumbled in her purse for her phone.

"Hello."

"Hey Jacqueline, how's your day going?"

"What do you need, Raphiel?"

"Do I have to need anything to check on my wife?"

"You never do when you are at work so I figured you wanted something."

"I actually wanted to know if you ate the breakfast that I left you and did you enjoy it?"

"Look, I'm grading my papers. I'll talk to you later." Jacqueline hung up the phone in his face.

⁒

Raphiel knew she was still a little warm by him not coming home until morning. Still, he didn't know she was this upset. Jacqueline had never hung up the phone in his face. She was usually the one who'd go the extra mile to make sure they didn't argue. He didn't know whether to call her back or leave it alone. He was his own man and he could do whatever he wanted to. She was going to have to learn that even if she had to learn it the hard way.

SHAYLA

Shayla cleaned up the cots she and her mother used in the shelter. Then she went to the serving table to fix them both plates. Today's meal was spaghetti, green beans, and a roll. She could hardly wait.

She loved the way the women from Ratman's Harmony House cooked. And spaghetti was one of her favorite meals. They prepared meals like her mother used to before she became ill. Shayla missed those days but hanging on to them wasn't good for her. She carried the plate to her mother and decided she'd better feed her mother first before she ate.

After lunch on Saturdays, the shelter made the people leave and they could come back after five. For some reason, Mr. Ratman asked Shayla to help the ladies in the kitchen today. She wouldn't have dared to say no because now she and her mother could stay at the shelter all day. She had some homework she needed to finish for Mrs. Vance's class. Most of the other teachers, she never did their work. Mrs. Vance never got crazy with her even when she got out of line. There was something different about her and it showed.

She was the only teacher who acted like the people at the shelter; she showed love. After she finished helping out in the kitchen, she took out her math book and began to do her homework. Right after lunch, her mom would fall asleep and she didn't abandon the routine today. *Praise Jesus my baby is asleep.* She was on the sofa snoring hard and this was fine for Shayla. She could finally get something done.

.

JACQUELINE

Jacqueline realized this was her first time hanging up on Raphiel. She knew hanging up on him was well out of character for her so she picked up the phone and dialed his number. Like normal, Raphiel didn't answer his cell phone which was beginning to become an annoyance to her as well as the late nights. She then decided to call his secretary to see if he was in his office.

"Hello, Vance's, the dealership that is certain to make you smile."

"Hi Auntie, is Raphiel in his office?"

"He was but I do believe he stepped out. How are you, Jacqueline?"

"I'm fine. Just a little upset but I know God will handle that too."

"He sure will, baby. Whatever you're going through, give it to the Master."

"I will and I love you, auntie."

"Me too, baby and I'll tell that knucklehead nephew of mine to call you when he gets back."

"That's okay, I'll see him when he gets home."

"All right, love, goodbye."

"Bye." Jacqueline hung up the phone.

BRADLEY

Bradley grabbed his little girl by the hand and took her to the passenger side of the car. He opened her door and buckled her into her seat belt. After he lost Denise, he was always cautious about Denisia in cars.

He purchased soft teddy bears to wrap around the seat belts in his car so she'd be comfortable. He even bought some for Mrs. Burch's daycare vans for all the children. If it had not been for the seatbelt, he would have lost Denisia too.

After he finished buckling her in, she gave him a warm smile and replied, "Thank you, Daddy." His little girl was always too polite and he had to thank Mrs. Burch for it. She took pride in teaching Denisia how to act like a little lady. He'd also had his First Lady, Denisia's youth leader, to thank. Both women took it upon themselves to teach his little girl the things Denise would have if she'd been alive.

As they drove to the theater, Denisia asked a million questions. Ever since she was three years old, she became quite inquisitive. Some of her questions shocked the crap out of Bradley but he did as any dad would do. He answered her questions and prayed she wouldn't ask why or how. When they drove into the theater's parking lot, she began to clap her hands in excitement.

"Daddy! Daddy! Are we going to see *Adventures of the Rock Stars?*"

"Yes, Denisia." He pinched her cheeks.

"Yeah!" she hollered to the top of her lungs.

Bradley decided he'd better buy their popcorn and sodas before they went into their movie. He couldn't help but blush as he watched his daughter beam with anticipation. She made her request known. Every time she saw the commercial on television and today, he'd honored her request. After he purchased their popcorn and sodas, he grabbed her by the hand and led her to their movie.

JACQUELINE

Jacqueline couldn't help but wonder if Raphiel had made it back to the dealership. She started to call him back but decided he'd be all right until after the movie. There were children everywhere with their parents and for some reason, she felt out of place. She even wished she would have brought her neighbor's child with her.

As she gathered her papers to put back into her tote bag she heard a deep voice say, "Excuse us." When she looked up, she froze. Why? She didn't even know. She'd never been the lustful type, but was something about him. He was a very distinguished gentleman and with him was the cutest little girl trying to pass by.

"Oh, I'm so sorry. You're excused," she said.

"If it's okay with you and no one else is sitting in these seats, we'll sit in these two next to you."

"Sure, no one is sitting there. I was beginning to feel like an outcast."

Bradley chuckled. "Are you here alone?"

"Yes, I decided to see how these rock stars were going to rock." And they both laughed. Jacqueline turned her attention to the middle man who was staring right into her face. "Hi, young lady, you sure are a pretty girl."

She grinned. "Thank you," and extended her hand for a handshake. "My name is Denisia and my daddy's name is Bradley."

"Please to meet you Denisia and you too Bradley," Jacqueline said, shaking both of their hands. "My name is Jacqueline," she announced, as the lights began to dim and the previews were getting ready to play.

"Hope you enjoy the movie," Bradley said with a cute smile.

"I'm sure I'll be rocking into tomorrow." And the two adults chuckled.

Jacqueline couldn't help but wonder where the mother was. She would have been too meddlesome to ask but that didn't stop her from wondering. What was a man as handsome as Bradley doing alone with his daughter at the movies?

Was his wife like Raphiel, too busy to come? Is she like Raphiel? Soon the music began to play. All the children including Denisia were laughing, clapping, and dancing in their seats. Jacqueline felt the burden of child-lessness creeping into her heart. She wanted to be a mother so bad, but God for some reason hadn't blessed her yet.

Bradley tried to sneak a peep at Jacqueline. She seemed to be enjoying the movie as much as Denisia. He noticed her wedding ring, so he didn't have to wonder about that. When she extended her hand for a handshake, he also noticed how big the diamond was. What he didn't know is what man in his right mind would let a woman this beautiful go to the movies alone. *If she were his, she would never have to sit in a movie by herself.*

She kind of favored his grandmother, who was African American and Indian. She had beautiful curly hair. Her nose was keen but made her facial features even more attractive. She looked like she was a basketball star by height and a model by face. He missed a huge part of the movie, thinking about her. Then, Denisia interrupted his thoughts.

"Daddy, I have to go to the restroom," Denisia said with her head tilted to the side.

"If you trust me and she doesn't mind, I'll take her," Jacqueline said. This would give her an opportunity to ask the little girl about her mother. Yes, she was being downright nosey, but sometimes you should be.

"Something tells me I can trust you and she seems excited about you taking her," Bradley responded. So Jacqueline grabbed the little hand extended to hers and they walked down the stairs.

"Ms. Jacqueline, do you have kids?" Denisia asked and it shocked Jacqueline that she remembered her name.

"No, Denisia, I don't have any of my own but I do have some I treat like my own. I am a school teacher."

"I'm ready to go to school but now I go to Mrs. Burch School. She teaches me everything and on Sundays, I go to Mrs. Strong's Sunday school class."

"That's great. Denisia, where is your mommy?"

"My mommy is in heaven with the Lord. She's up there watching over me and Daddy every day."

"She sure is, darling," Jacqueline responded, feeling a lump of sadness tugging at her throat. Here was a little girl who had no mother and she was a woman who wanted to be a mother but had no child.

"Ask your dad to let you come spend some time with me if you'd like."

"I'll ask him," she said, washing her hands and grabbing a paper towel. Jacqueline was so impressed by the little girl. She was so polite and her mannerisms were better than some of the teenagers she taught.

"Okay, I'm ready."

"I am also; let's get you back to your movie and your daddy."

"Yes, ma'am." Jacqueline grabbed her little hand and led her back to the movie.

"She didn't ask you a million questions, did she?" Bradley asked when they made it back to their seats.

"No, she didn't."

After their movie was over, Bradley and Denisia offered to walk Jacqueline to her car. Bradley carried her tote bag while Denisia carried her pen bag. She told Bradley that Denisia told her about his wife and for his loss, she was sorry.

After he told her what happened and about the miracle of Denisia being born, she couldn't help but shed a tear. Bradley assured her God had it all in control and he was blessed to have had Denise in his life as long as he did. Jacqueline was jealous of the faith in God that Bradley had.

She only wished her husband trusted God half as much as Bradley did. Raphiel rarely had anything good to say about God. When she started talking about Him, she could tell he didn't care to hear it. He'd go to church with her one Sunday out of the month and that was enough church for him.

MRS. BURCH

Mrs. Burch made it to Faith Temple to gather for Saturday afternoon teachers meeting. After all the Sunday School teachers arrived. She opened up with prayer.

"Father, we thank you for this is another day You have made and we are rejoicing as we are glad in it. We thank you for allowing us to assemble in your house of worship together again. Now Father, as we get ready to study Your word, allow Your Holy Spirit to enlighten, teach, and impart unto us. We desire supernatural wisdom about Your word. In Jesus's name, we pray, amen."

"Good afternoon, ladies and gentlemen," Sis. Burch said as she smiled in recognition of her teachers. Everyone was at the teachers meeting and they all were on time. "Sister Ford, can you read our lessons out loud?"

"Yes, Sister Sunday School President, our topic today is, 'It's All Good,' and it's coming from Philippians 4:11-13. Our summary scripture is coming from that fourteenth verse. It reads, 'I can do all things through Christ who strengthens me.'"

"Amen," Deacon Thomas said and others began to clap.

"Our summary reads as such. We live in a world where people never seem satisfied. They often go to God asking for things but not out of necessity. God said He would supply all our needs and like the birds in the air, some things we don't even have to ask Him for. Then why is it that people are not content? If they have no money, then they're unhappy. If they have a lot of money, they're still unhappy. Happiness comes when we receive wisdom and wisdom teaches us to be content with what we have and who we are. We say, "I thank God that I'm not what I used to be but I'm not where I ought to be," but in fact how do they know where they ought to be?"

"Amen," some of the teachers shouted.

"No one except for God has you where you are in life. So, we must learn to embrace the now and get all that God has for us to learn. In order that when He does move us, we'll be content in whatever state we are in. Whether we are in a place of humble necessities or complete prosperity. Whether we have all that we need or lack most of what we need. Sister Sunday school president, that is our summary." Sister Ford said and then she took her seat.

"Are there any remarks on the lesson?" Sister Burch asked.

"Yes, Sister President, I do thank God for the times. You know when I reviewed this lesson, I considered all the complaining folks I run into daily. Some folks are never satisfied and here we find Paul, satisfied in whatever state God had him in. Somehow we must allow Paul to be our example," Brother Boone said with his wife agreeing to every word.

"You're right. Somehow we must learn to be grateful," Sister Burch said. "I teach the toddlers every day at the daycare to say, "Thank you". You know, I know some grown folks who need lessons on saying thank you. We all need the spirit of thanksgiving. The Bible tells us to enter God's gates with thanksgiving. Then why do we enter it with, I need."

"You know, that's a question that we can ask ourselves." Sister Boone, the mother of Pastor Roderick Prince Strong inserted. "Why do we come to the throne for stuff instead of sometimes to say we are thankful and grateful."

"To be honest, sometimes I wish I was in a better place. Especially in my finances. Then to be honest about it, I'd spend most of my money doing God's job," Deacon Jones said.

"You're right about that. God would have someone in a faith lesson waiting on Him to pay their bills. Then here we come; the one with money who won't give when the Holy Spirit tells us too. But we'll break our neck trying to fix problems that God ain't told us to fix," Mother Pearl blurts out but everyone agrees.

"These are all good points. Now what I'd like you all to do in your classes is to make the students understand why it's important to be grateful. I also want you to emphasize the importance of understanding God's hands. And the fact that God will give us all the strength to endure all things." Sister Burch told the teachers. Then she asked Deacon Thomas to close the meeting out with prayer.

After he prayed, they all fellowship a little while longer and then they left the church.

RAPHIEL

Raphiel knew exactly where Jacqueline would be now. After he made a few stops, he drove his car to the theater and circled the parking lot until he found her car. There were no open parks on the row she was parked on so he parked in a spot a couple of rows behind her. He had a great view of her car so he wouldn't miss her when she came out.

Raphiel began to smile as his beautiful wife came out of the building. Then he noticed a gentleman carrying her tote bag. A little girl walked with them with what looked to be the bag Jacqueline carried her pens in. He started to get out of the car and go to where they were but he decided to watch them. He felt himself getting angry as he watched how attentive to his wife the gentleman was.

Then he saw Jacqueline hand the little girl one of her information cards. The little girl swung her arms around Jacqueline's legs and Jacqueline bent down and kissed her. Then the man gave her a handshake and they waved goodbye as they walked to the man's Mercedes. Raphiel could tell by the car the brother drove that he wasn't a broke fellow.

Whoever this dude was, he was well put together, and his little girl was almost the cutest little girl he'd ever seen. He couldn't help but wonder what type of relationship Jacqueline had with this man. Then, how could she love on someone else's child but wouldn't even give him one? When he turned on his ignition to leave the parking lot, he realized Jacqueline had spotted him. Reluctantly, he drove over to where she was.

"Hey, Raphiel, to what do I owe this pleasure?"

"Jacqueline, don't play with me. Who was that man and child?" he asked with a stern look. Jacqueline flinched a little as if she could see the spirit of jealousy all over him.

She was glad Bradley and Denisia already left the parking lot. She wouldn't have wanted them to see the man she married acting like this.

"You can't be questioning me. Not the man who thinks because he's grown he can do whatever he likes. Well, darling, saved I am, but a fool I'm not."

"I never tried to treat you like a fool."

"You might think you haven't, but you have. But you know what?"

"What?" he asked, almost not wanting to.

"I've put you in the hands of the Lord. Whatever is going on with you, it'll come out in the wash, and all I'm asking the Lord to do is sustain me."

"There you go with all that Lord mess. You aren't the only one who can ask God for something. As a matter of fact, if I ever see you with that guy again, I'm going to have to ask the Lord to keep me from hurting you and him."

"Now, I know you didn't threaten me. Raphiel, I've let you do many things but that's not something I am going to stand for. You can stay out until the next morning and you think you have the right to pick my friends. Well, darling, in case you don't know, I'm saved and satisfied. You don't seem to be either."

"I don't care what you say. You heard me, Jacqueline, and I'll see you when I get home." And then he sped off.

JACQUELINE

Jacqueline wasn't the least bit concerned about Raphiel. In fact, she thought it was cute. For the first time in their marriage, he realized he wasn't the only one who was grown. Never in her wildest dreams would she imagine that seeing her with another man would light a fire in him like this.

She thought she should have done it sooner although nothing about this day was planned. Bradley was a kind gentleman and he respected her as a married woman. She intended on being friends with him and Denisia. Because if the Lord didn't mean for them to know one another, He would have never made it possible.

Jacqueline turned her car on by the push of a button and backed out of the parking lot. As she passed by the restaurant, almost next to the theater, she spotted Bradley and Denisia going in. She realized she was hungry too. They were good company so she swirled the car in the direction of the restaurant. Both of them were as happy to see her as she was to have spotted them.

Bradley stood and pulled her chair out when she walked over to the table they sat at. He hadn't been in the company of a woman in a long time but this woman was the wrong woman. He had no desire to be with another man's wife but she was so friendly.

They had so much in common. Especially the fact that they were both saved. After they'd eaten and Denisia ran to the children's play area, they talked.

"So tell me, why isn't your husband with you?"

"Bradley, he left the parking lot threatening me. Raphiel used to be a good guy but something is going on with him. I can't put my finger on it."

"Jacqueline, it's not meant for you to put your finger on. God will show you whatever He needs you to see in His timing. Pray about it."

"Bradley, I've prayed and instead of getting better, things are getting worse. The bad part is Raphiel got saved and now he seems to be in a backslider frame of mind. I don't know what happened to make him stop trusting and believing in God."

"Jacqueline, men don't look at it like you all do. You know sometimes it takes a while or for something to happen for men to run to the Lord. I was out there hanging with the fellows and doing my own thing when Denise was alive. It wasn't until the Lord took her from me that I started believing. You know some folks will run from the Lord when bad things happen but I ran to the Lord. I knew anyone who could take one life and sustain another life in the same body, deserved to be honored, praised, and loved. So you see, some men are different."

"I understand but it sure would be nice to have someone who believed."

"I know but look at it this way; God is allowing you to go through this so you'll see His glory. Pray the Lord saves your husband and believe, God will do it."

"Okay. You've opened my eyes to a lot today, and I know our meeting wasn't by chance."

"Nothing can happen to children of God that He doesn't intend or permit. He allows us to go through some things and it's those things that make us who we are. Stay prayerful, Jacqueline and go through what God has ordained you to go through."

"Thanks, Bradley. I needed this."

After they finished sharing stories, Bradley got Denisia and they all left. It had been a blessed day in more ways than one. It seemed as if

God sent Bradley to encourage her in her most high faith. She wasn't looking at the situation with Raphiel like she was before their conversation. Finally, she saw the enemy for what he was worth....a complete hindrance in her husband's flesh.

When Jacqueline made it home she felt pleased with how her Saturday had gone. On other Saturdays, she'd come home a little hurt because she'd been alone all day. Today was different. She'd had the company of such a kind man and a beautiful young girl.

Bradley was different from Raphiel. Although she didn't know him, his kindness was impossible to hide. She wished Raphiel could have taken some lessons from Bradley on how to love his wife. Although she knew that would never happen, she knew someone who could get Raphiel to see how much she meant to him. *The Father.*

RAPHIEL

Raphiel was so upset by what he'd seen until he had to go and get himself a drink. He considered himself a responsible drinker but tonight he didn't care. As he sat at the bar thinking about Jacqueline, he was certain she was getting ready to leave him. She had every right because whether she knew it or not, he'd been up to no good.

"Lord, how did I get myself caught up like this?" he asked then turned his drink up until the glass was empty.

Then he wondered if the Lord actually knew his voice. He hadn't prayed in years because, in reality, he had no need too. Everything in his life was going well. He had a great business, a beautiful wife, and all the money he'd ever need. He tried making Jacqueline quit her job as a teacher because he made enough money to support her and a child.

She was so convinced that her being a teacher wasn't about her. 'It is about purpose,' she'd argue, and never took him up on the offer to become a housewife. She felt like her God had put her at Yorkwood High and she wasn't going to leave until He moved her.

What seemed to be a perfect life was turning out to be far from perfect. Raphiel was so caught up in himself until he started doing things he promised he wouldn't do. As he watched the couples dance, he wondered what happened to his marriage.

There was a time when he and Jacqueline would go dancing at the clubs together and have a ball. When she decided to give her life completely to the Lord, going to the clubs was the first thing she stopped. Then she stopped cursing and drinking the occasional glass of wine she used to. It was if she changed right before his eyes and there was nothing he could do about it.

At first, it bothered him that they seemed to be traveling on separate roads. Then he got so caught up in the dealership until he became numb to the pain. She did special things to show her love for him like cooking dinner, buying cards, and sending flowers. None of that mattered. It was like she was doing these things because she knew how unhappy he was beginning to feel.

Nothing could change how he was feeling. None of her gestures of love fazed him. She was pushing him out and he was going to get out. That's when he started going to the clubs and bars almost every weekend. Then, he started staying out much later than normal. Then something happened he would have never imagined would happen to him.

BRADLEY

"Hey, Mrs. Burch, this is Bradley."

"I know who you are. Where's that baby girl?"

"She's in her room playing with her dolls."

"Is everything okay?"

"Yes, ma'am, I needed to tell someone about our day."

"All right, I'm listening."

"Sister Burch," Bradley called her name. She knew it was something serious when Bradley went to the Christian side of things. At church, he either called her Sister Burch or Mother Burch, but at home, it was always Mrs. Burch.

She got quiet and Bradley knew what she was doing. Praying. He talked and she prayed.

"Denisia and I went on our daddy daughter date today. At the movies, we ran into a woman by the name of Jacqueline. Sister Burch, this was the prettiest woman I've ever seen. Well, since Denise."

"Okay," she responded, waiting on the but she felt in her spirit.

"She talked with Denisia and me and even had lunch with us. I ended up imparting into her life but I didn't want to. I wanted to tell her to leave the cheating man and come be with me and Denisia. It's like when I finally find a woman who I can relate to, she's married."

"Son, you know she's off limits then."

"Oh, yes, ma'am, I'd never cheat with another man's wife because we reap what we sow.Besides, my heart hurts for her. It's like he's taking her completely for granted and doesn't even care."

"Well, tell me, what can we do about it?"

"That's why I needed to talk to you. Sister Burch, she's saved and she believes in the power of prayer because I asked her. I want you to help me lift Jacqueline up to the Lord. I know God has some great things in store for her. She's so kind and she's deserving of a saved husband. Let's pray that the Lord will save her husband."

"Are you sure we need to be praying for him and her?"

"Yes, ma'am, they are one and if we pray for her, we need to pray for him."

"Bradley, you never stop amazing me. Boy, the Lord is maturing you and I can't do anything but shout...THANK YOU JESUS! It's when you pray for others that the Lord blesses you and you are next in line. God is preparing the woman that will be your wife and the mother of your child and more children. Believe that and stand on His Word and His promises."

"Yes, ma'am, I do believe it."

"Bow your head then boy and let's pray. What's her husband's name?"

Bradley patted his chin with his finger. "She said his name was Raphiel."

"Okay then. Heavenly Father, we come together touching and agreeing by way of the Holy Spirit. First, we want to thank you, Father, and say hallelujah to Your holy name. Now, Lord, you told us to pray for one another, so tonight we lift up Jacqueline and her husband Raphiel. Father, you know all about them, you made and created them in your image. Have mercy on them, Father. Satan, the Lord rebukes you concerning them. The Lord rebukes you concerning their marriage. We come against you and plead the blood of Jesus on them; from the crowns of their heads even unto the souls of their feet. Have your way God in their lives. Now, Father, I pray a special blessing over Bradley tonight. Keep him Lord even when he can't keep himself. Show him the woman that you are preparing for him and continue to mature him in Your word. We love you, Lord. I pray for a hedge of protection around Bradley's house and everything about him and Denisia. Let Your angels abide, protect, and keep them in all their ways. It's in Jesus's name we pray. Amen."

"Thank you, Mrs. Burch. I needed that."

"Thank you for giving me the opportunity to touch and agree with you, Bradley. I love you son and kiss my baby goodnight."

"I will and I love you too. See you at church tomorrow."

"Goodnight," she said and hung up the phone.

Bradley was certain he'd done the right thing. He didn't know what would happen tonight to Jacqueline but now he was confident she'd be okay. Judging from what she'd told him about Raphiel, he didn't know what to assume. All Bradley knew now is that the peace of God would rest in her midst.

RAPHIEL

It was a little past nine PM when Raphiel decided he'd better be getting home. He got up, dressed, and brushed his hair before going to his car. When he finally got to his car, he saw Clarence Larkins, one of his wife's students. He only knew who the child was because he'd approached them at the grocery store a couple of times when he worked there. He didn't know if the boy recognized him so he decided not to say anything but not the child.

"Hey, man, aren't you Mrs. Vance's husband?"

"Yes, I am, and how are you?"

"I'm not doing as fine as you, but it's all good," Clarence said, grinning like he knew something he shouldn't have known.

"Good seeing you," Raphiel responded before jumping in his car. Only God knew what this child had seen and if he'd tell his wife. Raphiel sped out of the parking lot. He couldn't risk losing all he had because a dumb child decided to tell his business. He decided to turn around and go back because with his life hanging in the air, he figured he'd better do something.

"Hey, kid," Bradley called out to Clarence and beaked for him to come to his car.

"Look, you never saw me." He dug in his pocket. "Here's a little package to secure that," Raphiel said, handing Clarence a hundred dollar bill.

"Man, you're crazy. You better come a little more correct than this. I saw what time you came and I saw exactly where you went," Clarence said, being the skilled hustler he was.

"I'm going to give you another bill but you better not say anything or I'll."

"You'll what?"

Without saying anything, Raphiel lifted the compartment between his seats. That's where he housed his shiny black pistol. Clarence's eyes widened because he knew exactly what Mr. Vance was suggesting. Then Raphiel sat his gun in his lap.

"I don't have to say anything, young man. It's clear you've been in the streets a long time and you know exactly where I'm coming from."

"Yes, sir, you won't be hearing anything about this. But you know what? I'm feeling so sorry for Mrs. Vance. She's such a good person and I know she doesn't know the kind of monster she's married to." Clarence said as he walked back to the crowd of older guys he was hanging with.

Raphiel couldn't believe he'd done what he did. What in his right mind would make him threaten a hood boy like that? This boy had a father who was no doubt as hood as he was and would destroy him. Shoot! Why did I have to go back over there? I should have carried my butt home. Of course, now, it was far too late for questioning and now time for deciding.

When Raphiel made it to his home, the home he'd built from the ground up, he sat in the garage thinking. If he decided to divorce Jacqueline, he knew he'd have to find another place to live. No judge in their right mind would give him the house. He loved her too much to even consider putting her out anyway. Why him? Why now? Were things so bad with Jacqueline that he should be considering divorce? He knew too well if Jacqueline ever found out what he was doing, she'd divorce him without questions.

JACQUELINE

Jacqueline had finished eating an apple when she heard Raphiel pull into the garage. She wondered if everything was okay. He'd been out there for ten minutes already and still hadn't come into the house. She thought about going out there to see what was going on but decided she'd better wait until he came into the house.

She went into the bathroom to wash her hands. Then retrieved her nightgown from the huge closet located on her side of their bathroom. Raphiel had her secret closet custom design in their master bath. She'd never forget the day she walked into their new home.

"Baby, come on. Let me take you to our new home."

"Okay Raphiel, but can you tell me something about it. You wouldn't let me in the plans and now you're blindfolding me."

"It's a surprise baby. I wanted you to see that I know what you like and I plan on giving you the world."

Jacqueline stood still in a blindfold. She'd never imagined the beautiful house she would soon behold. Finally, he pulled the blindfold from over her eyes and tears ran from them. Raphiel had the two-story home built in gray brick. There was a beautiful bay window on the right front that was one of the views from their kitchen. When he carried her in his arms into the house, the first thing she saw was the rounded staircase.

In the center of the foyer was a huge glass table with a gigantic vase. It contained her favorite flowers. A beautiful arrangement of white magnolias. To the right of the staircase was the first entrance into their kitchen.

The kitchen was so huge until it stretched from the front to the back of the house. It contained a breakfast area in front of the bay window. There was a big glass window that allowed you to see the view of the bay from every angle.

It was her dream home. He'd gotten everything right. From the blue tile on the kitchen floor to the beige tile that adorned all four bathrooms. She explained how she wanted her dream home to look on their first date, and he hadn't forgotten. Jacqueline was the happiest woman on earth that day.

No one could have told her she'd be spending most of her time in her dream home alone. Some days, she felt all she had was Jesus, her job, and her home. Raphiel was hardly ever home and when he did make it on some nights, it was still as if he wasn't there.

"Lord, I guess he's not coming in tonight." She said as she pulled her gown over her head. Then she grabbed the long socks that she wore on nights she slept alone. As she was about to leave the bathroom, she heard the alarm chime that he'd finally opened the washroom door.

Raphiel had the alarms set on every door. On the monitor screens in their master bedroom, it showed exactly what door was opening. The only way you couldn't hear when someone came or left is when Raphiel disarmed that particular door.

He'd been doing that quite a lot lately but what he didn't know was Jacqueline never slept hard when he was away. How could she? In a home almost as big as four homes, it was hard to get comfortable being alone.

YOLANDA

Yolanda had an exciting weekend. Now all she had to do was prepare her clothes for the next week. She'd taken out everything she thought she was going to wear and threw it across the ironing board. She ironed on Sunday after she'd gotten her Sunday dinner from her mother's.

This Sunday, she decided to stay home in case the man she was falling in love with came over. After she took another bat, she put a couple of rollers in her hair. Then she turned on her television to watch a little television.

After a couple of hours of old sitcoms, she decided she would go out for a drink. She put on her nice little black dress and draped a wide red belt around her waist. Then she took out her red hobo bag and a pair of red pumps out of her closet. Her closet was much too small for all the stuff she had in it, but she couldn't afford a house right now.

Her apartment complex was a high-class apartment. The exception was the nurse who'd move in the next building with her thuggish sons and brother. Yolanda had made it her business to call and report every time she saw them hanging out. To her, they were acting as if they were on a street corner. They'd gotten plenty of warnings, but nothing progressed. The woman's brother was an attorney so the apartment manager decided she'd better not harass them.

Yolanda grabbed her keys and journeyed to her car parked on the outside parking lot by itself. She wasn't about to let someone put a scratch on her brand new convertible Mustang.

THE GANGSTA & SHAYLA

He shouted until spit escaped his lips. "Girl, come here. I said come here!"

"What do you want? Can't you see I'm working?"

"Young man, she said she didn't want to come and you have to leave the premises right now!"

"Says who?"

"The police and I said so."

And before he could say another word, the police had his hands behind his back in handcuffs.

"Young lady, has this man been harassing you?" the officer asked. She knew she had better say as least as possible. He'd been to jail before and every time he got out, the person who put him there ended up dead.

"No sir, he wanted me to go out and I didn't feel like it," she answered, failing to look the officer in the eyes.

"Well, as she said, she doesn't want to go tonight and she isn't. Now if we get called back we are taking you to jail. Do you understand?"

"Yeah, I hear you."

"You better make sure you hear us and if this man tells you to leave the premises, you better run."

"Or else."

"Or else, you'll see."

"Now you have five seconds to get out of here."

RAPHIEL

Raphiel walked into the kitchen and poured himself a glass of wine. Jacqueline didn't allow him to drink anything except for wine in the house. She wasn't too particular about wine either. She felt that drinking went against everything she thought was right. Her reasoning for that was when people got drunk they forgot all aspects of what was right or wrong.

He never agreed with her. But Raphiel figured since he was hardly ever at home, she had the right to make demands about the house. After he finished pouring his glass of wine, he quickly downed it. Then he walked upstairs wishing she were already asleep.

"Hey Raphiel, how was your day?" she asked as she did since they dated.

"It was okay, I guess. All was fine until I saw you coming out of the movie theater with that guy and little girl. You seemed so happy with them but yet, you won't even give me a child."

"Why do you always try to put that on me? For whatever reason, God won't give us a child, not me. I don't have the power to give life or as a matter of fact, take one. People think they make babies because they have sex. I don't care how much sex you have, if God doesn't intend on you having children, you never will."

"Yeah, yeah, yeah, how many times will I have to hear you say that? But I see you have no explanation for the happiness I saw in your eyes today."

"I don't because, for the first time in years, it was like someone went to the movies with me. I'll never cheat on you, but because I married you, doesn't make me stop socializing with nice people. I do have self-control, Raphiel. Sometimes I question if you do." And before she could say another word, Raphiel hit her so hard across her cheeks until the whole room went black.

She tried to get up off the floor but her head was spinning. She laid down and prayed that head and ear would stop ringing. Jacqueline felt something warm running from her ear and her nose. She reached up with her hand to swipe the liquid. Blood. At the same time she noticed it was blood, Raphiel did too. He raced into the bathroom to retrieve a hot wet towel.

"Oh, Jacqueline, I'm so sorry. Baby, I never meant to hit you."

She hurt so bad but with every ounce of strength she had, she replied, "Yes, you did."

Raphiel could hardly believe his ears. Did Jacqueline think this bad of him now? Would him hitting her become his norm? He helped her to her feet and then he walked her over to the bed. She cringed as if she didn't even want him touching her. As soon as his hand left his side, he knew he'd made a big mistake. He should have never hit her. "Jacqueline, I'm so sorry. I never meant to hurt you."

"I never thought you would, but you have and now I want you to leave."

"I don't have anywhere to go, Jacqueline."

"Why don't you go where you've been spending your nights? And go before I call the police," she said as tears streamed down her face.

He knew in his heart, their marriage was over. Things were too far gone to make them better. The reality was now slapping them both in the face. Raphiel packed him an overnight bag and got a couple of outfits. Jacqueline meant exactly what she said. He didn't want a record with the police because he'd built his reputation upon everything that a convict was not. He glanced at her lying in their bed crying her eyes out, and then he left.

Raphiel didn't think he'd feel the pain he felt but he'd known for quite some time he wasn't happy anymore with Jacqueline. He'd tried blaming what he felt on her inability to get pregnant but knew things were much deeper than that. He wanted the Jacqueline he fell in love with; the woman who'd hang out at the clubs and dance all night long.

He wanted the woman who would give him mad passionate sex filled with dirty words. Instead, she was now saved. Everything he loved about her, was everything that went against who she'd become. He set all the alarms to every door and window and then he left.

THE GANGSTA

"Hey man, I got a job for you."

"What's up?"

"Somebody went and threatened one of mine and you know that won't work."

"Yeah, boy, tell me who, what, and where."

"The cat's name is Dead as far as I'm concerned. You meet me on the set and I'll take care of everything else. I got a little token that I need to retrieve from a shorty house."

"All right, you know I got you, my boy."

"First, it's that stupid — girl who had the nerve to defy me. It ought to be her but I'm gonna get her later. The cops would figure it was me. So I'll let her ride for some days. But this cat, he did all the riding he needed to."

YOLANDA

Yolanda went to the bar and when she got there, she spotted her Mr. Do Her Right sitting at a booth alone. She knew something was weighing on his mind so she decided to leave him alone for a moment. When she saw he'd almost finished his drink, she had the bartender make him another one.

The waitress took the drink over to where he sat. She placed his drink on the coaster and then turned and pointed at Yolanda.

It didn't take long for him to request her to come over. After they danced a little while and had a couple more drinks, he followed her to her apartment. When they got there, the same crowd of young men who were out earlier was standing around. He walked out of his car and then proceeded to help Yolanda out of hers.

The guys standing out watched them. She could tell that Raphiel was trying to decipher if it were anger or jealousy in their hearts. He pulled his bags from the trunk and closed it. Yolanda grabbed her man by the hand and pulled him in the direction of her place.

Bringing his attention back to her and off of them, she leaned in and smacked his lips with hers. *Now, focus on me.* She didn't have time to deal with no thugs and the fact that most of them carried guns made her eery. Had Raphiel said one thing to them, anything could've happened.

As they climbed the stairs to her apartment, she threw her hips a little harder. Her plan: set the stage for what is to come. He had never stayed overnight with her, so she had to wow him. She didn't think twice about the thugs looking at them the way they did. Yolanda was about to do as Missy Elliot suggested...get her freak on.

JACQUELINE

When Jacqueline finally woke up, she felt like she'd been in a hurricane. Her ear was still ringing and her head hurt like never before. She slid out of bed, went to the bathroom and peered at herself in the mirror. Her cheek was still a little swollen, but thanks to the bag of ice she put on it, the swelling had gone down a lot. She didn't care what people at church thought, because if she ever needed the Lord before, it sure was now.

She'd always said if Raphiel ever hit her, it was over and she meant that. As she dressed for church, she decided to wear a dress that had a matching hat. She thought the hat would keep people from noticing her face. Her speech was a little slurred too. Jacqueline figured she could leave early. If she left right before the benediction, she wouldn't have to explain.

When she made it to the church grounds, she began to shed tears. She was so grateful to be able to make it to the house of the Lord. From the foyer, she could hear Pastor Hunt singing "Amazing Grace." He didn't sing until right before he was about to preach so she figured the Holy Spirit had ushered him to do otherwise.

Her pastor had the voice of an opera singer and anytime he sang, it sent chills up and down her spine. She made her way in the sanctuary and took a seat on the back pew. She wanted to be as close to the back door as possible so when she left, no one would notice.

"Praise the Lord Saints." And all the saints of God hollered, "Amen!" "I don't know about you all, but I know it was God's amazing grace that's brought me. Did it bring any of you?"

"Oh, yes it did!" Mother Perow shouted as she stood and tossed her handkerchief toward the pastor. Everyone knew that when she got happy, she'd throw you if you were in her way.

"I know it's a little early, but the Spirit of God is leading me to bring the word. Somebody must be going through and need a word from the Lord." And the crowd screamed, "Amen!" While others bellowed, "Oh yes."

"Go with me in the word to 1 Peter 5:7. For your hearing I will be reading verses six and seven. And the Word of God reads," "Humble yourself, therefore under the mighty hand of God, that He may exalt you in due time. Casting all your care; for He careth for you."

"My subject today is, 'No matter what you're going through, remember God cares for you.'"

"Hallelujah!" someone shouted from the middle of the sanctuary.

"If you go back a couple of scriptures, here you'll find Peter giving instructions to the elders. Then he gave them to the young men. It is in verse six that he opens the scriptures to every being: male or female. He starts in verse six by saying, "Humble yourselves." God needs some folk who are walking in humility. If you humble yourself under God's hand, then wherever He leads, you'll follow. Can I get an amen?" He asked and the people said, "Amen!"

"God does not need us telling Him, He desires to tell us. It's something about going through. When we go through, we want to derive all kinds of plans to free us from the circumstance. When we go through we forget about God's will. Some of us go through in order for God to get our attention. He allows some of us to go through in order for us to become humble. "

"You are right about it!" one of the old church mothers yelled.

"Yes, God has blessed some of you with the desires of our hearts until it has become all about you. You've forgotten God has the power to give and He has the power to take away. Can I get a witness? I need you to know that humility can cause your going through--to get gone. When you tell the Lord, you need Him, He'll come through. See a humble soul doesn't mind calling on the name of the Lord when they're going through. I heard the Word saying, 'Weeping may endure but for a night, but joy comes in the morning.'

Endure for a little while and in due season, God will exalt you. He'll exalt you above the situation. He'll exalt you above your marital problems. He'll exalt you above your heartaches and pain. Anybody had to ever go through? Oh look back and see where the Lord has brought you from. Can you taste and see that the Lord is good? He's good, church!" And he continued.

"Then he goes on to say, cast all your cares. Not some of your cares, but all your cares. Your heartaches only? No. All your cares. You mean to tell me God wants me to cast my marital problems on Him? My hard-headed children? These bills that keep rolling in month after month? Yes. He wants anything and everything. Give it to Jesus. The Lord cares about you and He knows what you are going through. He wants to bring you out. Has anybody ever gotten brought out? Do you recognize how the Lord spared your lives? If you know that He cares for you, why don't you stand on your feet and give God some praise."

Jacqueline couldn't help but stand and clap her hands. She knew last night could have been worse than what it was. She knew all too well, she could have been dead. It wasn't Raphiel who spared her life, it was the Lord. She had a reason to praise his name. As soon as the pastor opened up the altar for an altar call, she ran toward the front of the church. She needed the Lord and she needed to cast all her cares at the altar. When she made it to the altar, she kneeled down and cried. Pastor lifted her to her feet and he wrapped his arms around her.

"It's all right, daughter. God knows Jacqueline and He cares."

"I know, Pastor," she managed to say but that didn't stop the buckets of tears that flowed from her eyes. She felt like a well overflowing. Then as the pastor held her in his arms, he began to sing the song she led.

"There's a sweet, sweet spirit in this place, and I know that it's the spirit of the Lord." The more the choir and congregation song, the more strength

Jacqueline seemed to get. When the pastor felt like she was strong enough, he gave her the microphone. *"Sweet Holy Spirit"* flowed from her mouth like a melodious awakening.

Everyone in the church was on their feet and some cried, while others shouted. There was a breakthrough in the house and Jacqueline received hers. She came to hear a Word from the Lord that would resurrect her broken heart and she got it.

She understood God cared about her. After church, she didn't break for the back door to avoid her church family. She realized she didn't have any shame or any reasons to carry guilt or shame. As she was about to leave the sanctuary, the Pastor called out to her.

"Daughter, do we need to talk?" he asked in that firm daddy voice he used with his daughters in the ministry.

"Pastor, I guess it would be good to tell someone what went on," she answers as she swipes away the tears. As much as she didn't want to cry, the tears forced their way out.

"Meet me in my office and tell my secretary I told you to go on in."

"Okay," she said as she walked to the back of the church to go to his office. When she got there, his secretary told her to go on in as if she'd already seen her face and knew why she was there. Jacqueline walked in and sat at the round table where he usually held conferences. His desk filled with books and study material made Jacqueline realize why the man was so smart.

He was not only a spiritual pastor but he was also an intellectual pastor, teacher, and instructor. His style of ministering in itself was a representation of the Holy Spirit. He could make you understand words you've never heard before. Something about his teaching caused you to desire more. She turned around and looked at all the books he had on his bookshelf. Some written by authors she had never heard of, and some authored by people who left a legacy of books. She took a deep breath as she dried her eyes. Then the door opened and the pastor walked in.

"Daughter, can you tell the pastor what's going on?" He asked with concern buried in his facial expression and love in his voice.

"Pastor, last night Raphiel came home and we were talking. To make a long story short, I went to the movies yesterday, by myself as usual. Even so, there was a gentleman there with his daughter and we talked. By the end of the movies, we'd become friends. He was a nice saved gentleman and never got out of line with me once. He knew my marital status and I don't believe he was there looking to pick up a woman. He and his little girl walked me to the car. I gave him my business card and told him that I would spend some time with his daughter if he needed to do other things."

"Daughter, where is the child's mother?"

"Bradley told me she died in a car accident three years ago."

"Okay, proceed on."

"Raphiel came to the theater and saw Bradley and Denisia walk me to my car. He assumed we were together. Now here lately, he hasn't been coming home until the next morning most of the time."

"Are you saying he's been out until twelve in the morning?"

"Pastor, he hasn't been getting home until three and four in the morning. I know without a shadow of a doubt that he's been with another woman. I can usually smell the perfume on his shirts. Pastor, I've never mentioned it to him. I figured if he didn't love me enough not to cheat, he'd get real sloppy and then tell me himself."

"Jacqueline, why did he hit you? I assumed that's why your cheek looks red and bruised."

"I told him I'd never cheat on him and because I'm married to him, that will not stop me from socializing with nice people. He drew back and hit me so hard until I felt like everything was black. Pastor, I would have never thought in a million years Raphiel would hit me. Our marriage hasn't always been the best and that's been because he worked so much. He said he worked so hard to give me the things that I want but in reality, there is nothing that I want. He works for himself and the business has become his cover to cheat."

"Well, daughter, don't jump to conclusions. Ask him if he's cheating before you assume the worst."

"Pastor, I know. You always told us not to be crazy. So, guess what? I'm not. I know that I know he's been cheating. With whom, I don't know but I'm sure it's someone who's as low down as he is."

"Jacqueline, so what are you going to do?"

"Pastor, I put him out last night. I always told Raphiel if he ever cheated on me, or hit me, our marriage was over. I know then he didn't believe me but when I told him to get out last night, he saw that it wasn't a joke. I will never be able to love a man who hit me. My father never hit my mother and if he knew, he'd try to kill Raphiel."

"You're right about that. He's been my deacon forever, it seems. I know exactly how he'd react. Still, he is your father and if it were my daughter, I'd like to know. Take a day or two and get you some rest. I'll bring you and your parents back here on Wednesday night after bible study."

"Okay Pastor. Well, I guess I'll let you get some rest. After that word, I know you're exhausted."

"Well, it's my job. I thank God He's given me the strength to do it for this long."

"I love you, Pastor, and I'll see you on Wednesday night."

"I love you too, daughter. Remember God cares and I do too. If you need me before Wednesday, I'm here in the office from eight until five. Because of the wife's orders, I leave on time every day." And he laughed a hearty laugh.

Jacqueline decided she did need to tell her parents and she wasn't going to wait until Wednesday. Her father would be furious to find out what happened between her and Raphiel in the pastor's office. He wouldn't or couldn't use profanity there because he respected the man of God too much.

She loved her parents and knew they loved her; she was not about to let this situation come between her and them. It would hurt them to hear the news in front of someone else and she would tell them but not now. Jacqueline needed some time alone to process what happened. She also needed time to sort through all the other things destroying her marriage. Deciding to go home and rest, she got into her car and headed in the direction of home.

When she pulled up in the driveway, she saw Raphiel's car. She started to pull back out the driveway and leave but the thought of running scared changed her mind. No man would ever intimidate or scare her, regardless of who he is or what he's done. Being careful, she did what any smart sister would have done, she dialed 911.

"Hello, this is 911, how may we help you?"

"Yes, this is Jacqueline Vance and I live at 402 Columbia Trail. Would you send an officer out to escort my husband off the premises?"

"Did he hit you?" the operator asked.

"Yes, and I asked him to leave and not come back."

"Ma'am, stay in your car and the officer is on his way."

"Thank you," Jacqueline said before hanging up the phone. She didn't know why he was here and didn't even care. All she knew is that she wanted him away from the house and that was that. Raphiel hadn't noticed that she'd pulled up because if he had known, he would have come to the car. Still, she was more comfortable in the car and glad that he didn't know that she was there.

When Officer Jones arrived, she smiled. Although he looked familiar, she couldn't recall where she knew him from. But having someone familiar meant not having her business shared.

"Hi, Mrs. Vance, when I got the call, I thought it might've been you. I'm Officer Patrick Jones, Sherell Jones's father, and my child loves you."

"Hi, Mr. Jones, I apologize for not recognizing you. I have so much going on in my life right now. How's your family?"

"Everyone is fine and I understand. We go through sometimes but we still must thank God for going through. It's these through times that allow God to know if we trust Him."

"I know you're right about that."

"Can you give me a little heads up on what happened?"

"Well, he came home last night and we had a little argument. Then, he hit me. Raphiel has never hit me before so I know something is going on. I don't want him to go to jail, Officer. Jones. I only want him to leave the house until I'm comfortable."

"Okay, Mrs. Vance, why don't you let me go in to talk with him and then you come in a little later?"

"That's fine, I know the alarm is on so the number is 4451."

BRADLEY

Bradley got up, dressed, and then dressed Denisia for church. He was always excited about the messages his pastor would bring. He woke up on Sunday mornings anticipating and anxiously awaiting for what God had in store for him.

Pastor Roderick Prince Strong, Senior Pastor of Faith Cathedral Temple was deep. Bradley admired how he shared the deep things of God with his congregation. While listening to Pastor Strong, no matter what it was or where it was in the Bible, he could take you there. If it was on the boat with Peter and the storm was unruly, listening to him made you feel like you were there too. After he finished putting the finishing touches on Denisia, he escorted her to the car.

She was as eager as he was to get to church on Sundays. First Lady Strong had a way of making the youth, even the toddlers, desire more of God. He put Denisia's seat belt on and then went to his side. It was normal for his neighbors to be on the porch drinking coffee on Sunday mornings. He threw up his hand to greet them.

He'd spent hours trying to persuade them to visit his church, but decided that they weren't ready. He'd planted the seed and someone else had to do the watering. It would definitely have to be Jesus to save those folks. He turned his dial to KOKA to listen to the Sunday Gospel Express radio show.

Whether you were ready or not, when they started to play those church songs, you almost walked in with your hands up. When they arrived at Faith Temple Cathedral, he smiled. The church was beautiful and the color of the flowers was different again thanks to the First Lady. She was faithful to the church, her family, and the flower beds. Faith Temple was a beautiful place inside and out and he was proud to be a member of such a great church.

"Hallelujah. Hallelujah. Hallelujah." The choir sang as he and Denisia walked in the door. They were about to start the intercessory prayer segment and he was happy to be in the midst. He kissed Denisia and told her to go on to the children's church and she smiled and left. Bradley moved to his seat and then kneeled down for a word of prayer.

"Lord, bless this service. Bless the man that is going to bring Your Word. Please forgive me of my sins and trespasses before you. I desire a pure heart so that it may receive Your Word and will honor it as a seed sown from You, Lord. I love you Lord and I'm here expecting You to move, in Jesus's name. Amen." Then he rose up off the floor and joined in with the choir. "Thank you, Jesus. Thank you, Jesus." He sang with passion and gratitude because despite every up and down, he thanked the Lord.

Sister Burch went to the microphone to intercede. Bradley got excited because he loved hearing her pray. After she finished Mother Pearl, followed by Deacon Jones, and then Sister Sheila. By the time Sister Sheila finished, the church was already on fire. Then the praise and worship team took the stage.

Their first song was a song his late wife Denise wrote. She had been the church music director since she was seventeen years old until the day she died. She wrote most of the church's praise and worship songs and still to this day, FTC sang her songs. Today, they did Bradley's absolute favorite and he sang right along with them.

"I'm standing at the well with you, Jesus. I'm standing at the well with you, Jesus. I'm standing at the well with you, Jesus. Oh, Oh, Oh, here's my cup. Lord would you fill it up. I don't want... to ever thirst again."

Mother Pearl always did the lead for this song. There was something about her voice that sent chills through Bradley. He thought about Denise for a moment and then his mind went to Jacqueline. He felt like for the first time since Denise, he'd found a friend in a woman. He knew the enemy was trying to rise up to raise stuff in her life but he also knew this was the trying of her faith. A testing to make sure that her patience was in tack.

Bradley whispered a little prayer for Jacqueline. After he said, 'Amen,' he brought his whole and undivided attention back on the praise and worship team. After worship was over, the pastor stood up and everyone in the congregation stood to their feet. He was dogmatic about people reverencing God and his congregation knew how he felt. He turned the pages of his Bible, and once he stopped he glanced over the crowd.

"There's a heavy need in my heart to open the altar for prayer this morning. Is there anyone here who needs the power of prayer to go to work in their life or in the life of family or a friend?" Before he could even finish asking the question, Bradley and a few others made their way to the altar.

Pastor took the anointing oil out and put some on his hands. Then he went from person to person. Some got slain in the Spirit and some left crying. When he made it to Bradley, Bradley whispered to him the name Jacqueline.

Pastor Strong began to intercede for Jacqueline. He came against every demon and ill trotted spirit that was trying to wreak habits in her life. Then he commanded God's angels to surround her and take her over the storms. As if he needed more reinforcement, he asked the church to join in prayer for Jacqueline.

Bradley got worried because he knew that his pastor walked in the mantle of the prophetic. If the pastor prayed this hard for Jacqueline, something was about to happen that she had no control over. She was going to have to stand despite everything going on in her life. After they finished praying, Bradley didn't know if he was lighter or heavier.

He wanted to hear from her but he knew that wouldn't be good. He still had to consider that she was a married woman. There could never be anything between the two of them. After service was over, Bradley went up to shake Pastor Strong's hand. He had yet again given a soul-stirring message that penetrated the debts of Bradley's heart.

Today's message, "The Danger of Not Knowing How Much God Loves You," was better than the one from last Sunday. That message entitled "The Danger of Not Knowing Whether You Love God," also had stirred his heart.

When Denisia came running over to him, he'd known by her jovial mood that she'd had as good of a time as him. She was waving her drawing and going on and on about the Bible verse to learn for next Sunday. Bradley smiled thinking how proud Denise would've been. Her daughter knew scriptures and had learned her first Bible verse when she was two years old. With the help of Mrs. Burch, she knew a whole lot more.

Denisia saw her favorite lady, Mother Lucy, and tore away from him to go hug her. Bradley's first instinct was to run right behind her, and he did. Even at church, you could never be too careful watching over a child. He waited until she and Mother Lucy finished their conversation, to scold her.

"Baby, you can't snatch away from daddy and run away. Okay?"

She looked up at him knowing full well his voice was low but he was yelling. "Yes, sir," Denisia said, looking sad.

Bradley pinched her cheek. "It's okay little girl. Next time, tell Daddy and I'll take you to see whoever you want to see." She smiled and wrapped her arms around his leg.

Bradley scooped her up in his arms and carried her to the car. He felt safer carrying her across the parking lot instead of her walking. It was his highest and most important goal in life, to keep his daughter safe.

Sister Burch invited Bradley and Denisia over for Sunday dinner and he'd accepted. He was planning on taking Denisia out to eat, but a home cooked meal was better than any meal ever made. He'd tried cooking dinner a few times but Denisia was always so picky. She never seemed to want the things he wanted and he was sick and tired of hamburgers. She knew not to say what she didn't want around Sister Burch. She had sense enough to know that when it came to Sister Burch, a child did and ate whatever she told them too.

When they made it to Sister Burch's house, the smell of her good cooking seemed to have met them at the corner. Bradley could smell the greens and cornbread as soon as he opened his car door. The outdoor grill had the entire neighborhood smelling like good old smoked meat. Bradley couldn't wait to get his hands wrapped around one of those chicken legs. Sister Burch also had the best potato salad known to man. She fixed everyone a plate and then Brother Burch said grace over the food.

Brother Jacob Burch was a kind man but he was also a man of very few words. He and Sister Burch were complete opposites. Bradley figured that's what made their marriage last for thirty years. There wasn't too much talking going on while they ate because everyone was too busy tearing the food up. Sister Burch did what the old folks called putting her foot in the food. She was a good cook and eating her food was like feeling her heart. You could feel the love in every bite.

YOLANDA

'Mr. Do You Right' left Yolanda's apartment and walked in the direction of his car. He didn't notice the four guys dressed in black parked across from his car. He was too busy trying to get wherever he was going until he failed to notice his surroundings. He jumped in his car, started it up, and left.

What he didn't realize is that he wasn't the only one who left. The car trailed him a couple of cars behind, but they watched his every move. They were going to get him if it were the last thing they did. So, with patience and ease, they followed.

JACQUELINE

"Mrs. Vance, are you sure you haven't gone in the house yet?"

"No, I haven't. Mr. Jones, as soon as I saw his car under the garage, the first thing I did was call 911."

"Hold on. Stay out here for a little while." Without another word, officer Jones got on his radio. He called for the homicide detectives. Jacqueline could tell that something wasn't right because he turned his back to her as he used his radio. She strained to hear him but the only word she could make out was detectives. Jacqueline could feel something awful creeping in her stomach. She didn't know what to do so she did what came natural, she prayed.

When the other officers arrived, three of the detectives went into the house. One stayed outside with her. There were policemen all over the place and about six squad cars parked in front of her house. As one of the detectives asked her to go sit in the back seat of his car, she saw the coroner's white van.

Jacqueline immediately started screaming. She didn't know who but someone in her home had to be dead. She prayed that it wasn't Raphiel. She didn't know if he'd committed suicide or what. *Lord did I drive him to kill himself? Did my Daddy find out he hit me?* All sorts of questions were swirling around in her mind. When she ran to the door, one of the officers picked her up by her waist and took her back to his car.

"Mrs. Vance, what time did you make it home?" The detective questioned Jacqueline.

She started feeling nervous and nauseous. "I made it home about 2:15 today." Her voice was shaken by a flood of emotions. Feeling like she was about to emit everything she'd eaten for breakfast, she closed her eyes to breathe.

"Mrs. Vance, are you alright?"

Jacqueline laid her hand on her stomach and nodded.

The officer moved a little closer to her. "We are going to take you down to the police department to get you away from all this. I can assure you that everything will be fine. We need to get you out of here before the news cameras get wind of what has happened."

She looked at him with pleading eyes. "Officer, please tell me that Raphiel is all right. Please tell me."

He placed his hands in position to catch her if she fell. "Mrs. Vance, your husband has transpired. Why don't you call your family to meet you down at the station?" And before she could say another word, the detective told Lt. Jones to carry her to the downtown station.

When they got into the squad car, Jacqueline cried. By the time they passed the Lakeshore exit, she looked over at Jones. "Mr. Jones, please tell me something."

He looked at her with compassion, but all she felt was fear. "Mrs. Vance, I'll have to wait until we get some family with you. Give me your parent's number and I'll call them."

Even the tone of his voice told her it was bad. After a complete meltdown, Jacqueline gathered herself. She quoted what she called her go-to-scriptures.

After she glanced out the window, she looked back at the officer with renewed strength. "Please call my Pastor first and tell him to go and get my parents. If you don't mind, I would like you to tell them to call Raphiel's aunt as well. His parents are no longer with us but his aunt is like a mother to him."

"I will. You sit there and try to calm down. We'll be at the station in a little while."

"Okay. Oh God, why Raphiel? Why now?" And she buried her face and wept.

BRADLEY

Bradley made it to his immaculate home and put Denisia down for a nap. *Cleanliness was next to godliness.* He could hear his mother's voice saying anytime their surroundings got cluttered. To keep from hearing her scolding voice, he made sure things stayed neat.

There was something extra hard about doing that on Sundays. If he wasn't changing into two different shirts, he was changing her dresses. Then, after service had to fight with getting things back together when all he wanted to do was watch a game or sleep. Mother Burch had schooled him on how to prepare Saturday nights for Sunday morning. She'd made coming home a blessing after church instead of a dreadful event.

Bradley looked down at the sleeping beauty in his arms. She was so tired until she didn't even make it to the corner of Sister Burch's street before she fell asleep. She ate and played so hard that the events had worn her completely out.

He smiled as he laid her in the top bunk where she slept most often. Bradley took the blanket with photos of Denise he had special made and covered his baby. *Sweet dreams, my princess.* He kissed her and went straight to the kitchen.

Pushing the button to start his Keurig, his plan was in motion. Make himself a cup of coffee, sit down, and watch a few games, the perfect Sunday after service plan. He turned on the television, and then placed his coffee Yeti in the armrest of the recliner sofa. Bradley unbuttoned his dress shirt, as he heard a breaking news alert. In the past that would have been his clue to turn the television right back off because he detested the news.

After Denise died, Bradley watched the scene of her accident over and over again. Every news channel and social media reported the wreck but he didn't find out until someone called him. They'd shown Denise's mangled car on the news and everyone knew more than he about the accident.

Months after he buried her, he vowed not to watch the news ever again. He'd done well up until today. Something deep on the inside was telling him not to turn the channel. As he searched for the remote he heard...

"Good evening, there's been a body found at 402 Columbia Trail. We don't know all the specific details. From what we've heard, the wife came home and called 911 to have her husband escorted from the premises. When the officers arrived they found the victim in a pool of blood, next to a letter."

"Lord," Bradley said.

The reporter continued. "The police haven't given the details about what is on the letter but an inside source claims that we'll know more soon. Police are asking if you have any leads or know anything, please call 1-800-FIND-HIM. We will be updating you with information as soon as it becomes available. This is Shanice Thompson with KVET back in the studio."

Bradley hurried to his bedroom to retrieve his wallet. He pulled out the card that Jacqueline gave him to verify the address. He knew as soon as he heard the broadcaster say the address that it was Jacqueline's home. He'd read the card many times when he got home.

Jacqueline also told him that her husband built her very own dream home in the Trails. The Trails was well known to any individual with goals. It was a very upper scale neighborhood where your finances had to match your goals. Doctors, lawyers, and other blessed and professional individuals preferred the area.

Bradley picked up his phone and dialed Sister Burch's number. He was glad she answered on the second ring. That told him she wasn't asleep and she wanted to talk to him. When she answered, he skipped all the usual formalities and went straight to the point. "Sister Burch, are you watching the news?" He tapped his table as he waited on her to respond.

Like in slow motion, she spoke. "Yes, Bradley, you're talking about where someone has murdered that man in the Trails?"

Finally, geez Louise, that took her forever. He and brother Burch had an inside joke. She always spoke in her slow instructor's voice which made her response rate to them horrible. "Yes, and Sister Burch, it's Jacqueline's husband."

"Say what? The lady you met at the movies, Bradley."

Nothing was funny about the moment but her response was. He low-key chuckled and responded, "Yes, ma'am."

She gasped. "Oh, God no."

"Sister Burch, where is she?" *I hope she isn't dead.* I restrained my tongue from saying what my mind thought. "I prayed and asked God to please not let anything happen to her."

"Come on Bradley. Child, please don't think the worst. Do you think she did it?"

Her thoughts are as bad as mine. "Sister Burch, I don't believe Jacqueline would kill anyone. She's saved and I know she is. I could feel the Holy Spirit in her voice and she knew the Word."

Sister Burch cleared her throat. I knew that whatever she prepared to say came with facts or hard reality. "Bradley, a lot of folks know the Word but that doesn't stop them from doing drastic things when they are angry. Anger is a natural response that will push or pull you into a sinful act."

This time he sighed and hesitated because she had a valid point. The jailhouses are the proof that saved or once good folks can do evil things. "I know that too, but not Jacqueline."

"All right, baby. Then come on, let's intercede for her."

"Yes, ma'am." I bowed my head and waited as Sister Burch began to pray.

HUBERT

As soon as they pulled into the police department, Cheryl and Hubert Collins ran to their daughter's side. Cheryl took her baby girl in her arms and held her as they both cried. Then Geraldine came in as broken as they were. She took Jacqueline by the other side. She and Cheryl led her into the waiting room that Officer Jones had prepared for them.

As they were about to turn the corner, Hubert caught a glimpse of his daughter's swollen cheek. He knew Jacqueline too well to consider that she'd killed him. Yet, something in the pits of his belly told him that Raphiel had hit his baby. He was waiting for everyone to stop crying before he began his series of interrogations.

As soon as Chief Carlos, who was the elder cousin of Officer Jones came into their room, he went straight to Hubert. "Hello there, Lt. Collins. How's retirement?"

"Oh, it's lovely and now this." Hubert ran his hand over his thick full beard.

"Yeah, I know," Chief Carlos Jones said, bending his neck so that Lt. Collins would follow him into his office.

Once they got into his office, Chief Jones motioned for Hubert to sit on the sofa. He then sat across from him in the matching letter chair. "Hubert, I didn't want to say this in front of your daughter. We've hid some things from her until we know what is what. There was a letter left at the scene." He handed Hubert his phone to read the picture he'd snapped.

'Since this punk wanted to cheat on his wife and make threats, I decided to make him eat his words.'

"So, you mean to tell me that Raphiel was cheating?" Hubert asked.

"From this letter, this is what we gather and from the looks of Jacqueline's face, cheating wasn't all he was doing." Chief Carlos Jones said wishing he didn't have to be the one who had to tell Lt. Collins this information. Collins was his lieutenant and he had grown to respect him. If it had not been for Collins, he wouldn't be Chief of Police now. Collins did everything he could to get Carlos in this position. And with Jesus and Collins on your side, nothing was impossible. "Tell me, did she see him like that?"

"No, looks like we got a call to 911 at or about 2:16. Jacqueline pulled under the garage and saw his car. He must have hit her last night because she told Officer Patrick Jones that she told him to get his stuff and leave. Even so, when she got home, he was there. She decided to call 911 instead of even going in the house and that proved to be the best choice she could have made."

"What happened when you sent your cousin out?"

"After we got the call, I knew it was Jacqueline's house so I let Andre go out there."

"Thank you, man. You know I owe you. Do we have any leads on the killer?"

"First off, I owe you my life, Lieutenant. All we know is that when Raphiel came home, the neighbors said that there was a black car following him. The neighbors said as soon as he pulled to the back in the garage, the other car pulled right in behind him. They didn't hear anything after that."

Hubert ran his hand over his beard again. "Without compromising the integrity of the investigation, is that all?"

Chief Jones looked at his friend. He would never treat Lieutenant Collins or his family as if they were outside the loop of law looking in. In all his years in law enforcement, he'd never met a more by the Bible book then law book abiding citizen. The only man who mentored both blacks and whites and no one had a harsh word to say about him. "No. One of the neighbors saw the car but said it sped off so fast she could only get the last four of the license plate numbers. She said she was going to write it down because the Vances never had company. That was her very first time ever seeing a car over to their home besides yours and your wife, and his aunt Geraldine's. This made her suspicious."

"Thank God we got that much otherwise Jacqueline would have been suspect. Have you questioned her yet?"

"No, we haven't. We figured you'd want to be here when we did."

"Okay. Well, let's get this over with. I'm going to take her along with my wife and Geraldine out of town until you all find out something."

"I was going to suggest the same thing."

"You know I know how these investigations go; better safe than sorry."

SISTER BURCH

"Father, You never said that weapons wouldn't form against us, but You said in Your word that they wouldn't prosper. Have mercy Father. Have mercy on Jacqueline right now in the name of Jesus. Father, we plead the blood of Jesus all over her from the crown of her head to the souls of her feet. Have your way, God. We bind and rebuke every spirit of death, destruction, and despair."

Bradley nodded his head in agreement.

Mrs. Burch continued. "We lose your angels of peace, Lord. Build her up now because we know she's torn down. Give her hope, Lord, when it seems like hope has vanished, in the name of Jesus. Now God, please do it now. Do it because we trust You, Lord. Do it because we believe you can. We wage war on the enemy, and still the hand of the enemy, in the name of Jesus."

"Thank You, Lord. Thank You for what You are doing right now. Thank you for giving her strength now God. We love You. We exalt You. Most of all we believe in Your word. Amen."

"Hallelujah! Thank you, Sister Burch. I know she's okay."

"Praise the name of the Lord. Praise the name of Jesus."

"Bless You, God. Hallelujah! Hallelujah!" Bradley shouted to the top of his lungs.

JACQUELINE

Jacqueline sat beside her mother who had begun to sing, "I Need Thee." It was an old Baptist song that Christians sang in times like the ones they faced now. With every stanza of every verse, she felt stronger. She loved Raphiel and now he is gone. She hadn't even had the time to tell him that she loved him. *Why didn't she try to make things up? Why did she make him leave last night?* These questions plagued her mind. Then out of nowhere she heard a voice say, "Life and death lie in the power of the tongue."

She'd heard the voice before and knew it was the voice of God. *But what was He saying?* She didn't know what He meant. *Did Raphiel say something that would make someone kill him?* She didn't know but she was going to find out.

Hubert strolled back into the room and walked right in front of his daughter. "Baby girl, you do know you'll need to answer some questions. Are you strong enough for that?"

"Daddy, I can do all things through Christ that strengthens me," Jacqueline announced. She'd watched her Daddy over and over again put his emotions aside to deal with important things. Despite his hurt, if it needed his undivided attention, that's what he gave. And she would be no different. Her Daddy's blood ran through her veins and she wasn't stopping until whoever did this went to jail or hell.

Hubert smiled and pulled Jacqueline from her chair and into his arms. "That's my girl. Now let's go to Chief Jones' office."

The only thing that helped her as she walked down the hall was knowing her daddy was right by her side. Of course, she'd been to the offices before, but all on the good side of the law. Not saying she was on the bad side now. But the facts are, she is as much of a suspect as anyone else.

When they got to the room, Chief Jones and two detectives awaited them. Jacqueline sat down on the opposite side of the table. Hubert kissed his daughter and went to sit at the end of the table.

Chief Jones looked at Jacqueline. " Jacqueline, tell us what happened last night."

"I went to the movies yesterday and Raphiel came to the theater. He saw me walking out with Mr. Bradley and his daughter Denisia. He assumed that I was enjoying another man's child instead of giving him one. We had an argument and I told him that I will never neglect socializing with people because I am his wife. He got angrier and hit me. Raphiel has never hit me before." Jacqueline looked straight in the eyes of her father when you made that last statement. She needed him to know that she would've never betrayed his trust by living with a man who hurt her.

Chief Jones jotted down some notes and then asked, "What happened next."

"I told him to get out and to take his clothes with him. After church I talked to the pastor about what happened. I was on my way to your house Dad, to tell you what happened but I decided to come home and take a nap first. When I drove up, I saw Raphiel's car. I did what you always told me to do, call the police." Jacqueline swiped tears from her eyes before continuing. "I felt like I didn't know what he would do so I'd rather be safe than sorry. Then Officer Jones came out and he went in. The next thing I know I saw the coroner's van and I knew something terrible had happened." Then she started crying harder.

Hubert got up from his seat and consoled his daughter. Sure, one would think that was favoritism, but to the staff it was nothing for him. Whether they were family or murderers, he treated everyone the same. If the criminal confessed their faults, he told them to seek the Higher Power for guidance. And he shared the importance of repenting and learning to heal to anyone who would listen. "Come on, baby girl, you're doing great. Can you tell your Daddy anything else?"

"As I was waiting for the police, I noticed that the trash can in the back was in a different place. Raphiel never moved the trash can because he never took out the trash."

"Okay. Sergeant Jones, call over to the scene and have them finger-print the trash can and look around it for clues."

"Okay, sir."

"Lieutenant Collins, that will be all for now. I know I don't have to tell you this but please take care of those ladies."

Hubert nodded. "I got them, Jones." He turned toward his daughter. "Until they find out who did this, I'm going to take you, Cheryl, and Geraldine away for a while. Come on, let's go share the news with those two."

Jacqueline felt even worse now. Because of her, their entire family had to go into hiding. By the time they made it back to the room where her mother and aunt sat, she was crying her eyes out.

Hubert shared the news with his wife and Geraldine and asked,

"Is everyone in agreement?" All three women, with teary eyes, shook their heads signifying that they were all in agreement.

YOLANDA

Yolanda watched the six a.m. news and then sipped her coffee before leaving for school. She saw the story about the murdered man in the Trails and figured he must have made a bad business deal. Getting to school wasn't anything she hurried to do but today was special. She had to tell Jacqueline that her Mr. Do Her Right decided to spend the night for the first time.

When she arrived at Yorkwood High, things were as crazy as usual. The only difference is that she didn't see Jacqueline's car. It was usually parked in the space right in front of the school. Jacqueline always got the best spot because she came to school so early.

I'm so happy I'm going to even speak to Brandon. "Good morning, Brandon."

"Good morning, to you, Ms. Clark."

"Uhm hum. Hope today isn't as crazy as Friday was."

"Me too, especially so you won't have to leave campus before time."

Yolanda coughed. "I guess I'm busted."

"Don't guess, Ms. Clark, know."

"Okay, sir. I won't leave before time, but it was my planning period and I had some planning to do."

"Good, Ms. Clark, if you're going to leave early, hit the time clock the next time. That is all I'm asking you to do."

Yolanda rolled her eyes. "I will," she lied. They already weren't paying her what she was worth. And if you asked her, a free hour was not in the least bit coming close to what she deserved.

"Have a blessed day."

Yeah. Yeah. Whatever. Heck I'm done talking and he's still running his mouth. "I don't know about blessings but I am going to have a day." *This is the very reason I don't speak.*

"Remember, you have what you say."

"Um hum," Yolanda said before darting around the corner. She'd made all the small talk she'd intended on making for one day. She had more important business to take care of. She opened the door to her classroom. After laying her things on her desk she hurried to Jacqueline's classroom.

"Hey, and who are you?" She asked in a nasty tone of voice.

"I'm Patrice Johnson and I'll be subbing for Mrs. Vance for a couple of weeks."

Yolanda put her hands on her hips. "Where the hell is Jacqueline? That heifer didn't tell me she'd be out. I'm going to call her after school and read her."

"Do what you do but as for me, I'd like it if you'd allow me to finish praying before class starts."

If this ain't some crap. Yolanda puckered her lips. "One holy roller takes a break and the same kind subs for her class."

"Call it what you'd like. I'm rather proud that I know there is a true, risen, and living Savior. Now if you don't mind. Oh, have a blessed day."

"If anybody else tells me that again, I'm going to snatch my hair out of my head." Yolanda stormed out the room and down the hall to Mr. Jacobs' classroom.

"Hey, did you know that Vance would be out for some weeks?"

Jacobs squinted his eyes and then pushed his glasses up on his nose. "Rumor has it that it was her husband that they found dead yesterday."

"No. You gotta be kidding me." Yolanda stood hoping it was a bad joke.

"Sure wish I was. They're keeping things hush, hush until they find whoever killed him."

"Oh, shoot! I know Jacqueline is a praying fool right now."

Jacobs laughed. "Yeah, you know she's always calling on the name of the Lord and if anybody knows Him as a keeper, it's Jacqueline."

"But I see that God didn't keep her husband from dying." *How could God do this to someone as faithful as Jacqueline? This is another reason for me to rely upon spirit and not on God.*

Jacobs interrupted Yolanda's thoughts. "I look at it like this, we all have a time to go. No one knows how they're going to go; we know where we are going."

She furrowed her eyebrows, "How do you suppose that?"

"If we believe in Jesus, we know hell won't see us." Mr. Jacobs said as if he were certain no other truth trumped the one he told.

"I guess. You folks believe in all that hogwash. I know Jesus is real but I don't understand how y'all do all y'all do and think heaven is going to be your home." Yolanda said with her hands now on her hip and her neck rolling.

"I rebuke that proud spirit in you young lady in the name of Jesus. We are sinners but know we're sinners saved by grace. We all have sinned and come short of His glory but all we have to do is repent. What about you?"

"Whatever, let me carry my butt back down here so I can get ready for my own little demons."

"Ms. Clark, the only demons you have are the ones living on the inside of you."

"I hear you, but I don't believe you." And with a snap of the finger, Yolanda turned around, snatched her head, and went back to her room.

JACQUELINE

"Dad, I'm feeling so bad. I need to be with my students and here I am feeling like a truck has run over my whole life."

"Baby, in life things happen. One day all is well and the next day you feel like you are standing in hell. The only thing we can be certain of is our belief in Jesus. If we don't know anything else, we know He was born, He died, He got up from the dead, and He lives."

"That, I know I'm certain of. What I don't know is why things always happen to Christians. I take my co-worker Yolanda, she doesn't believe in Christianity but she believes in Jesus. Things always seem to be going right for her."

"Jacqueline, don't fool yourself. Isn't that the same girl that's been jumping from man to man since you all were in college? Well, that's not right, so everything isn't going right for her. She's trying to find in these different men the security that comes with knowing Jesus. Baby, what seems right for man is the ways that lead to destruction. There's the spirit of witchcraft in the land and its total purpose is to make you deny the faith. Know that God doesn't allow things to be so unbearable until they overtake us, they elevate us."

"Dad, I know all these things. I'm hurting so bad right now. The last conversation that Raphiel and I had, I was putting him out. Now, I can't even tell him that I've forgiven him. Pastor and I had a talk. I realized that although our marriage was over, he was still my friend and I forgave him in my heart."

"Baby girl, that's all that matters."

"Jacqueline, he loved you." Geraldine said as she walked into the living room and right into the conversation. "He always thought that you didn't want him anymore after you got saved. He figured that you'd rather be with a man who was going to church every Sunday and he wasn't ready to make that commitment."

"Aunt Geraldine, you know I never pushed him. I knew that he believed and that was all I needed to know. Raphiel could never say that I compared him to any other man. Sure, I wanted him to go to church with me but I never pushed. I thanked God for the Sundays he did go."

"I know, baby. I know he wasn't perfect but he loved you, Jacqueline. He was going through a transition and he didn't even realize it. Satan was trying to keep him caught in his past, enjoying the things of the past, but God brought him out. God took him so that he wouldn't turn from his belief. God rescued Raphiel from himself."

"Thank you, Aunt Geraldine. I didn't know if you blamed me or not. I didn't know. You know God spoke in my spirit that life and death are in our tongue. I went back and forth in my mind trying to see if I spoke death on him. I realized while you were talking that God wanted him to have life. Before his tongue could cause him a death that would result in damnation, God took him. I know that God never fails and whatever He does, He does it with our eternity in mind."

"Excuse me, ladies," Hubert said before leaving the room. They nodded in recognition of his request.

"Do you know what you're going to do with the dealership? I know it's soon but the guys have been calling me all day."

"Auntie, I know you love that place. After Raphiel's funeral, I'm going to let you run the dealership. You know everything there is to know about the business and I know you'll take care of it."

"I sure will. I do thank you, Jacqueline. The dealership is all I have left to remind me of my sweet nephew."

"I realize that you must be hurting as much as I am. Aunt Geraldine, I don't hold you accountable. Anything that's happened between Raphiel and me is our fault and no one else's. I love you like my very own aunt and you'll never have to be alone. In fact, I hoped you'd move in with me. There's no way that I'll be able to stay in that house all by myself."

"Darling, thank you, and thank You, Jesus. I am all alone, Jacqueline. After my sister died, Raphiel was all I had. Baby, I would love to stay with you. We will get through this, Jacqueline. No matter what comes or goes, we will make it." And the two women embraced one another. While Geraldine kept Jacqueline busy, Hubert took his chance to check in with Chief Jones. He didn't want Jacqueline nor the other women worried about the investigation. He knew that any lead was a good lead and because they didn't see it that way, they would frustrate him. Hubert dialed the number to the chief of the police office and waited until the secretary picked it up.

"Hey, Sgt. Mitchell is Chief Jones in his office."

"He sure is. Lieutenant Collins, how is Jacqueline?"

"She's as well as either of us would be, I suppose. She loved that boy and even though I don't believe he was good enough for my girl, he was her husband."

"Yes, sir, I know how you felt. Chief is in his office and I do believe he was waiting on your call. Give me one moment and I'll patch you to him. May God bless you, Lieutenant, and we're praying for your family."

"Thank you, Mitchell."

"Hey there, Lieutenant, I was sitting here waiting for your call. We received some information about the case. There was a weapon found in the trash bin by the garage door. The one that Jacqueline noticed moved. We've brought the gun in and as we speak, the team is dusting it for prints. They're also checking the serial number to find out who it's registered to."

"So, you know if they left the gun at the scene, they weren't the smartest criminals. Unless it's a stolen gun or they're trying to frame someone else."

"You know criminals do strange things sometimes. Let's pray that we come up with some type of leads with what they've found."

"Thank you, Chief. You don't know how much this means to me."

"Lieutenant, as I've told you before, it's the least that I can do for you and your family. I'll call you as soon as I find something else out."

"Okay, don't tell the women who you are." And the two men laughed.

SHAYLA

Disappointment was on Shayla's face when she didn't see Mrs. Vance in her first-hour class. Although her teacher could rattle her nerves, she was the only person who gave her hope. It was all those long lectures about Jesus that Mrs. Vance had given her that made her feel comfortable.

She only wished she felt comfortable enough to share the things going on in her life. Mrs. Vance would have tried to help her. Yet, she remained silent for fear of her business floating all over campus. Especially, since Mrs. Vance was friends with the teacher she disliked most.

Students could always tell when teachers disliked them, because they had a way of picking. And some hated her and she knew it. Shayla had overheard Mrs. Macon talking about her with her English teacher Ms. Clark. She decided at that moment that she would give them all the hell she was capable of giving.

Today, she didn't want to fool with any of them. Of all days she had to deal with this crazy sub. Anyone who would write her name across the blackboard in big pink letters was crazy.

"Good morning, class," some of the teens shouted, "Good morning."

Shayla never opened her mouth and she wasn't about too.

"As you see, Mrs. Vance is not here. Until she comes back, I'll be your sub."

"When is she coming back?" Shayla asked and all the others chimed in.

"I'm not sure. What I do know is that whenever she gets back, she'll find her students behaving the same way they were when she was here."

"Okay then you can tell them to call me when she gets back and I'll be back."

Then Shayla put her things back in her tote and got up from her seat.

"Young lady, Mrs. Vance has her education. Unless you want to stay where you are right now in life, you better try to get yours. Education is the only thing that is going to change your life circumstances. Now if you don't believe that then you can walk out of this door, but I pray that you understand and stay here."

Shayla still wanted to go, but she thought about her situation. She'd been a mother to her mother since she was able to walk and talk but she wanted more. She took her things out of her bag and sat down. For some reason, Mrs. Johnson sounded a lot like Mrs. Vance. That's the same stuff Mrs. Vance used to get her to come to class. "All right Mrs. Johnson, I'm staying so you need to be starting whatever you're teaching us today."

"I'm glad you're staying, Shayla."

Shayla confirmed exactly what she thought. Otherwise, how did Mrs. Johnson already know her name? Mrs. Vance must have schooled her on me, she thought. She glanced up to see Mrs. Johnson giving her a wide smile.

She didn't attempt to smile back because she knew she'd been set up. Patrice Johnson was so happy that their tactic worked. Jacqueline called her late on Sunday evening. She'd informed her about every teen in the class. She'd also given her the rundown on little Ms. Shayla Smith.

"Patrice, there's a girl by the name of Shayla Smith in my first-hour class. She can have a nasty attitude at times but I know it's a hard shell to keep her from getting hurt."

"Jacqueline, do you think I can handle her?"

"Yes, I do. Tell her that her education is going to take her out of her present

situation. That's what is going to work. Whatever her situation is now, it's not a good one. When I talk about her education, it seems to give her hope."

"I hope it works for me."

"I know it will. You're a lot like me, Patrice. There's love in your heart for children and they know who loves them and who doesn't; especially, teenagers. You can say one wrong thing and they feel like you can care less. Some of those children have experienced things I couldn't imagine going through when I was their age. I pray in that classroom when they're in there or out. Often, when they're working I'm sitting at my desk praying. My father always said that the prayers of a righteous man always avail. It's a prayer that's going to bring these kids through."

"Thank you, Jacqueline. I'll be there in intercession at seven o'clock. You know I know what prayer can do. This girl seemed to like me when I was her age and you know I wouldn't change a thing. My mother's sickness caused me to grow up fast but I made it with the help of the Lord."

"You sure did, Patrice. I believed in you then and I have faith in you now. When Mr. Brandon asked who I wanted to leave my class with, he'd already called out your name before I could even answer. God already knew. Well, I better get going. If you need anything, call Chief Jones and he'll get in contact with me. I love you, girl."

"I love you too, sis. Look, we are all praying for you at the Star."

"Thank you. Goodbye." Jacqueline hung up the phone.

Patrice was eager to do a good job for Jacqueline. Jacqueline had been her role model. When she was in college, Jacqueline was the one who made sure she had money and all the stuff a college kid would need. Whenever her mother was out on a drug binge, Jacqueline always took her home with her. She could be a child there.

She and Jacqueline would go to the movies on Saturdays and out to eat all the time. She kind of treated her like her very own child.

When Patrice saw Shayla, it was as though she was looking at a mirror of how she used to be. She wanted to take the girl in her arms and hold her. No one had to tell her, kindred spirits were already visible. When she started the class on their assignment she went to her desk to write Shayla a letter.

Led by the Holy Spirit she let the teenager know that she would be there for her. As the class packed their things two minutes before the bell, she folded the little note in her hand. Then when the bell rang, she shook Shayla's hand placing the note in her palm. Shayla closed her hand around the letter and walked out.

HUBERT

Hubert fixed his usual morning breakfast for all three of the ladies. He'd cooked breakfast for Cheryl for forty-two years. She ate his food whether it was good or bad and so did Jacqueline. He was a little uncertain about cooking for anyone else. Geraldine must have felt his heart because she came in bragging on how good his food smelt. He fixed all three ladies plates and then he poured each of them an icy glass of orange juice. As he was about to fix his plate, his phone rang.

"Excuse me again, ladies, you all enjoy your breakfast while I take this call."

And he kissed Cheryl on her cheek before he exited the room.

"Hey, Chief, you got any leads."

"Lieutenant, you will never imagine in a million years who the gun belonged to."

"Carlos, you know not much surprises this old man."

"This will. The gun is the property of Yolanda Clark. You know the girl that went to college with Jacqueline and the one that teaches at the same school."

"What's that about? Do you think she did it?"

"I don't know, Lieutenant. All I know is the gun is registered to Yolanda Clark, and she purchased it over a year ago. She bought it from the gun shop at the corner of Texas and Wagner. The owner said she claimed to need it for protection since a new tenant came to live not far from her."

"Why would she need it then? Did that tenant say anything to her?"

"We have already talked to the apartment manager. She said Ms. Yolanda is always complaining about the young men at the apartments. She hates them hanging out at all times of night. You know. This is a case of an upscaled apartment tenant versus the new thug tenants. The woman's name is Hattie Hines and she has two sons and two brothers living with her. All are over the age of eighteen except one. One of the brothers goes by the name of T.J., which is short for Thomas Hines Jr.

"We've been watching this dude for years and I mean to tell you, the sucker is smart. His hand is on a lot of murders but we can't get him. The other brother is Terry Hines. He's in college and seems to be an okay kid. We've hauled him in on a couple of occasions about his brother and even though he complies, we never get much. Thomas has harassed her a time or two and she bought the gun for protection."

"So Yolanda bought the gun in case she had to use it on one of them."

"Yes, I do believe you're right, Lieutenant. But how on earth did that gun get to the scene of the crime? Were there any fingerprints on it?"

"This is the other thing that's going to blow you away. The gun not only had Yolanda's fingerprints on it, but it also had Raphiel's fingerprints on it."

"Chief, you mean to tell me that Raphiel's prints were on that gun."

"Right. So, I don't know if you're feeling the same vibes that I am or not."

"Could she be the mystery woman that the fool was messing around with? Did she kill him in a jealous rage or something?" Hubert asked.

"I don't know. What I do believe is that if she didn't kill him, whoever did it knew that she was the one he was fooling around with. You know, some around here are pointing to Jacqueline. They feel like she'd know how to frame a person because of you. I've tried to suppress their thoughts but you know how that goes."

"Yes, I do. Look, don't jeopardize your job. If I have to come out of retirement to solve this case, I will. My daughter is no murderer although, it seems like she could have had cause."

"I know that too, Lieutenant. I haven't brought Yolanda in for questioning yet but I do have a car close by to get her if you feel they should."

"Yes, get her in for questioning as soon as possible. I'm on my way there. Tell the officers not to make a scene at the school. Tell them to take her out the back doors if she doesn't resist. In fact, tell her that they're taking her to see Jacqueline. I'll call the principal who is a frat brother of mine and give him the heads up."

"Thanks, Lieutenant, I'll do that. Goodbye."

Hubert hung up the phone in disbelief. He couldn't believe that Yolanda would do such a thing to Jacqueline. Jacqueline had all but carried her butt through college. He had even sent money to buy a book or two for her when they were in school. He'd overheard Jacqueline and Cheryl talking about how she switched men.

He never would have imagined that one of the switches was his very own son-in-law. Hubert called Yorkwood High and asked to speak with Ronald Brandon. He and Brandon graduated from college together. They had become fraternity brothers when they were sophomores in college. Even though college for them had been years prior, they still were brothers in every sense of brotherhood.

"Hey, Ronald, this is Hubert."

"Man, I know who you are. How's our baby girl?"

"She's doing but she's not why I called. Is Yolanda Clark there today?"

"Yes, she is."

"One of our detectives is on the way to pick her up for questioning. I can't say much but I wanted you to know so that you could have your assistant find her a replacement for the day."

"You've got to be kidding me, Hubert. Jacqueline is one of the only teachers around here who even put up with her. Man, this is horrible. Do I need to call her downstairs?"

"That would be good. I've asked the chief to tell the officers not to make a scene. Prayerfully, she'll go because it's about Jacqueline."

"I sure do hope you're right. That girl is a time bomb. I do know that she doesn't have a clue that it was Jacqueline's husband on the news. She came in ranting about Jacqueline not being at school. She acted like she hadn't heard anything."

"She might haven't. She and Jacqueline don't hang out anymore since Jacqueline got saved. She's never been to Jacqueline's house and hadn't even ever met her husband; at least we thought."

"Okay, Hubert, I'll take care of things here. As a matter of fact, one of the officers walked into my office."

"Thanks, Ronald."

"Man, anything a brother can do for another brother deserves no thanks. That's what I'm here for."

"Me too and if you need anything from me, call."

"Later." Ronald Brandon hung up the telephone.

SHAYLA

Shayla opened the note in her next class, which was English. She didn't have far to go since she was across the hall in Ms. Clark's class. She took her seat so she could read what Ms. Johnson gave her. Then she began reading...

Shayla, I was once in your shoes. I had to care for a mother who was on drugs. No one told me but because you act like I did back then, I kind of figured it out. Mrs. Vance helped me a lot and she is the very reason why I went to college. Keep praying and God will give you the opportunity to go to her for help. God loves you and He will see you through. If you need me, I'll be here all this week. Love you, Ms. Johnson.

Shayla folded the letter and stuck it in her backpack. She wasn't about to tell anyone about what she was going through. They could be murdered and so could she. It was her problem and if God loved her so much, He would have made her mother get off drugs so she could be a normal teenager. She felt her eyes begin to water so she took her arm and drugged it across her eyes.

"Ms. Shayla, do you have a problem or something? I said all eyes on me."

"Ms. Clark, don't start with me today. I came in here, sat down, and haven't said one word. Don't start picking with me today because I don't feel like this."

"Who do you think you are? You are in my classroom and I can do whatever I want here!"

"Go to hell, Ms. Clark." And Shayla picked up her backpack and walked out of the class.

"The nerve. If either of you want to follow her, you can leave now." Ms. Clark said, with her hands on her hip.

"That won't be necessary," a voice coming around the corner said.

"Ms. Clark, you're needed downstairs in my office. Go on and Mr. Jacobs is going to watch your class. Shayla, take a seat where you sit," Ronald Brandon said as he watched Yolanda roll her eyes at the child. Then he stood aside as Yolanda Clark stormed by him. It wasn't his intent to upset her, but she was always filled with attitude. He'd wanted to fire her twice but each time Jacqueline had begged him not too.

"All right, class, I want you guys to be on your best behavior. Mr. Jacobs is on his way down. Like you are now, is how I want you to remain." Ronald Brandon said as he focused his eyes on Shayla, who seemed to be a little preoccupied. She was in tears when he met her storming from the classroom earlier. His mind went back to their conversation as he peered at her.

"Mr. Brandon, that lady has a problem. She's mad when I talk and when I don't talk. She is crazy, Mr. Brandon."

"No, Shayla, she's going through something. You know how you lash out when you're going through, there's no different."

"But, Mr. Brandon, I lash out at everybody, not one person. She's always on my back and I hate her."

"Shayla, hate is such a strong word. You don't hate her, you dislike her ways. See, that's the same thing I tell you when you are acting out. The teachers don't hate you; they dislike your ways. Now, dry your eyes and walk back to your class with me. Remember, I keep telling you that it doesn't cost you anything to be nice. The Lord knows what you're going through and He will fight your battles for you. All you have to do is stay in a child's place. Bless them that despitefully misuse you and hurt you. Okay, little girl."

"Okay, Mr. Brandon, but I am still tired of her."

"Shayla, pray for her. Okay. Is that too much to ask of you?"

"No, sir, I'll do it."

"Good girl, now come in here and go straight to your seat."

There was something about this kid that made him have compassion for her. He'd tried to explain to his teachers that kids go through like adults. He told them that often they don't handle going through like adults do.

He also told them to be patient with the children. To remember that teenagers experience challenges every day. He emphasized that some are now faced with being adults in their homes. Children have to work, take care of their siblings, and fight demons like adults.

Brandon felt that his staff was capable of handling children with special situations. Yorkwood High had children whose parents made less than twenty-five thousand a year. In order for a teacher to even consider teaching at Yorkwood, they had to love the inner city, at risk, hurting youth.

When Shayla noticed Mr. Brandon was staring at her, she smiled and her smile brought him back to the present. He'd never seen her smile and he thanked God that there was still some joy somewhere in this child. He gave her a wink and turned to greet Mr. Jacobs who was at the doorway.

HUBERT

Hubert said good-bye to the women and told them not to open the door for anyone. He waited until a patrol car was in front of the house and then he left. There were sharpshooters all over his land. If anyone dared to hurt one of these women, he'd made sure they wouldn't hurt anyone ever again.

As he drove down 3132, his thoughts were on Raphiel.

He couldn't understand why he'd chosen to mess around with someone so close to Jacqueline. For years he'd questioned Jacqueline about their marriage. She'd always made excuses for him and blamed everything on the dealership. He'd promised Cheryl he would let his daughter handle her own husband. It had taken everything for him to mind his own business, but now he wished he hadn't.

He never liked Raphiel from the beginning. There was something about him that made Hubert's stomach tighten. All his life he'd dealt with criminals, and to him, his daughter had gone and married the type of man he detested.

Hubert could feel his blood begin to boil. He turned on the relaxing sounds of Kenny G. Instrumental music had become his place of solitude. During his years at the department, he had to find a place of calm in the midst of storms. Times like these made him search his CD case for a place of retreat.

YOLANDA

Yolanda walked down the halls to go to Brandon's office. She didn't appreciate him coming to her classroom disturbing her. Nor did she like the fact that he let that girl back in her room after she'd got up and left. She was going to have a talk with him because he was overstepping his boundaries.

When she turned the corner, she saw two officers standing in Brandon's office. She thought they were looking for Brandon.

"Mr. Brandon isn't here, he's upstairs," she said, rolling her eyes at the officers.

"And you are?" one of the officers asked.

"I don't know if it's any of your business, but I'm Ms. Clark," she said, looking at him with piercing eyes.

"Well, Ms. Clark, actually we're here to see you. Could you come to go with us to the police station? We have a couple of questions for you," Officer Jones said.

"I don't know why you'd be questioning me. I don't have anything to do with cops. Now if you don't mind, I need to go back to doing what I came here to do."

"Ms. Clark, you are going with us whether you want to or not. Now I can arrest you and take you out in handcuffs but my boss instructed us not to make a scene. That is unless you don't cooperate," Officers James said.

Yolanda put her hands on his hips. "I don't know who you think I am. If you need to say anything to me, I'll have to call my attorney."

"Ma'am, you can call anyone you'd like at the station. Now, would you please come with us? I would hate for your students to see you in handcuffs," the officer said, smirking as he looked at the other officer.

"Whoever told you to do this must have gotten me mixed up. If you're going to take me, you better get the handcuffs. And know when all this is over, I'm going to sue the state for every penny I can."

She was something else. A feisty chick who wasn't about to budge. Officer James looked at Officer Jones, who'd already taken his handcuffs off his belt. He knew that he had to do something because Jones had enough of the woman's mouth. She was a whippersnapper as his grand-mother used to say, but she was pretty. James decided he'd better tell her something different.

"Ms. Clark, this is a matter about Jacqueline Vance. Now they tell us that she and you are friends. Right now she needs you and so do we."

"That's all you had to say in the beginning. Let's go. If Jacqueline needs me, I'll go wherever I need to go." She snatched her purse off the chair and looked back at them like they were moving too slow. When they made it to the station, they put her in a holding room so that Chief Jones could question her.

Chief Jones and Lieutenant Collins were behind the interrogation glass looking at her. The officers explained how she resisted until Officer James told her about Jacqueline. They said that even in the car she was trying to make them drive faster.

BRADLEY

Bradley woke up after his morning nap and fixed himself a cup of coffee. Then after he'd showered, he put on a pair of jeans and a sweater. The weather was beginning to get a little chilly because autumn was setting in. The leaves on the trees were turning beautiful shades of reds and orange and the wind was crisp and cool.

After he noticed he was a half hour late, he threw on his navy blue jacket and left the house. Luckily, his cashier, Michelle, was eager to get the extra hours. She'd been an employee of the liquor store since it opened. He hadn't told her, but he wasn't planning on staying today.

He wanted to show his face and see if she needed anything like: change, a break, or something to eat. He had put finding new employees on his agenda for the holidays. Tequila Delights was once a place he took pride in, and now it was a business he owned. He had even considered selling it but he only wanted to sell it to an owner that would contract his employees.

"Hello, Michelle."

"Hey, boss, I figured you weren't coming in today," she said, kind of sounding disappointed.

"I see you're disappointed that I did."

"No, sir, I'm not disappointed. I had kind of figured my check with the extra hours. You know Christmas is coming up and I have those children who want everything."

"I understand, Michelle. In fact, if you'd like, you can open and close the store all week. I have something I need to do. Now if you need help or a break, Janet King said she'd be able to come in with you. Call her when you're ready but try and give her at least five hours each day."

"That is not a problem. I'll call her to come in at three. After I've gotten my kids off the school bus, helped with homework, and cooked them some dinner, I'll come back at eight. By then, I could have even got them their baths and prepared them for bed. They can watch television until nine and then it is television off."

"Sounds like a plan to me."

"Okay, boss, you're the best," Michelle said, throwing her arms around his neck.

"You are too, Michelle. I thank you for being so faithful. I guess there's no better time than now to tell you that I'll be buying everything the kids want this year. Have them each make a list with five things."

"I know God put you and Denise and Denisia in my life. The day you all hired me, I knew you all were special people."

"I can say the same about you. Denise told me that you would be the best person for the job, and she was always right. Now don't forget if you need me, you can always call."

"I won't forget boss-man, and kiss Denisia for me," she said as he walked toward the door.

"See you tomorrow." And then Bradley ran and jumped back into his truck.

JACQUELINE

Jacqueline stood gazing out of the front room window. It had been so long since she'd visited her parents' ranch home. Everything outside was so enchanting. The leaves scattered all across the lawn and the sky was a misty blue, making the perfect canvas painting. It kind of looked like it was going to rain but although gloomy, the outdoors was still beautiful. She went to the closet to retrieve her jacket and yelled to Cheryl and Geraldine that she was going outside. She saw the cops in their places but that was normal.

She'd always had policemen around all her life. As she swung on the swing her dad put in the tree thirty-five years ago, she couldn't help but cry. She would miss Raphiel even though she rarely saw him or spent time with him. One part of her couldn't believe that he was dead and another part of her felt like he had died a long time ago. Their marriage hadn't been the same since her last miscarriage. She'd tried getting pregnant again, but God didn't allow it.

After two miscarriages, Raphiel's love and heart began to wax cold. He'd blamed her for the miscarriages and said her job was the main reason he'd lost his happiness. Jacqueline knew deep down that it was more than her job. She knew that the day she got saved was the day she lost her husband. Raphiel felt like he was competing with her belief and that was far from the truth. She'd never thrown up religion in his face. All she did was stop doing some of the things he loved to do and she'd begun to hate.

There was nothing special about going to clubs. She'd been drinking alcohol when she found out she was pregnant with their first child. She blamed the alcohol for her loss but Raphiel blamed her. Her mind drifted to how their marriage would have been if she could have had his baby. He'd still love her like he did the day they got married, she thought.

She buried her face in her hands. Then Jacqueline heard that sweet voice say, "Weeping may endure for a night, but joy comes in the morning." The words were comforting but they still didn't ease the pain. She wanted to tell Raphiel that she loved him and how she wished their marriage could have worked. How she wanted his child. Her words were now only thoughts of what would never be. He was gone.

Jacqueline began to sniffle and as soon as she looked up, she saw her mother coming toward her with some tissue. Cheryl sat down on the swing next to her daughter and wrapped her arms around her. Jacqueline began to cry even harder.

Jacqueline looked up as her mother approached her. "It's okay to cry, my sweet baby. Cry. God is going to bottle every tear you shed and when you get to heaven, He's going to show you that He got every tear you've cried."

"Thank you, Mama."

"Cry. Baby, no matter how Raphiel treated you, you still loved him. He was your husband and you have the right to cry. God is going to fix it and your heart will be lighter," Cheryl said, stroking her daughter's hair. "This too will pass and, Jacqueline, the pain won't last."

"Thanks, Mama. My heart is hurting so bad. I wish I wouldn't have put him out last Saturday night. Maybe, he wouldn't be dead."

"Jacqueline, you know we taught you that you have your name in the Lamb's book of life. Besides your name is the date you were born and the space for the date that you're going to die. No matter how hard it is on those around you when your day comes up, you have to leave here. The only assurance we have is our belief in the true and risen Savior.

Then, and only then will we have the blessed hope. To be absent from the body, is to be in the presence of our wonderful Lord."

"Yes, Mom but..." Jacqueline began to speak but Cheryl interrupted her.

"Now, Jacqueline, Raphiel's date came and he had to go. There was nothing you could do to stop it. Baby, I believed he loves you. The two of you were traveling on different highways; going the opposite way. You know two people who are unequally yoked rarely survive in a marriage. All you can do now is thank God that your day hasn't come. Then, Jacqueline, you must live your life as if your day might be tomorrow. Praise God for right now, baby. Thank Him for being a God who knows and won't fail."

"Thank you, Jesus," Jacqueline said, a little above a whisper.

"That's right, baby, praise your way through this."

"Thank you, Jesus. Thank you, Jesus," Jacqueline said over and over and each time she got a little louder and clearer. By the time she finished, she and Cheryl were both praising God. Now instead of a painful cry, they both were crying tears of joy.

"The Lord finds joy in His saints that praise Him in spite of what they're going through. That's why the Word says, "The joy of the Lord is your strength." Cheryl preached and continued on.

"As he finds joy in your praise, the more strength you get. If you never remember anything I've taught you always remember, praise will get you through."

"Okay, Mama. I won't ever forget," Jacqueline said, still waving her hands as an act of surrendering to God's will.

"You are never too far, that praise won't carry you through. Hallelujah! Hallelujah!" Cheryl began to shout loud and Jacqueline followed.

YOLANDA

Yolanda sat in the cold empty room wondering what was going on with Jacqueline. All she knew was when she got to school, Jacqueline wasn't there. That wasn't normal because she usually always beats everyone to school. The other teachers were engaging in their usual gossip seasons. But Yolanda never took part in them.

She figured if they discussed someone else's business, they'd discuss hers. She had one friend who never judged her no matter what, and that was Jacqueline. Although they never saw each other outside of Yorkwood, that was okay. Jacqueline had a husband and Yolanda didn't want to be in their way.

They were fine conversing on the phone and at school. Jacqueline was actually the only friend she had. She'd never been able to get along with females because no matter what, their men would always want her. She didn't have time for the cat fights anymore. She was beginning to become impatient but decided that since it was about Jacqueline, she had to wait. Then finally there was a knock at the door, followed by the twisting of the knob.

"Hello, Ms. Clark, my name is Chief Carlos Jones and I am the chief of police in this lovely city."

"Yeah, I know. I've seen you on the television before. What is going on with Jacqueline and what can I do to help her?"

"I'm glad to see that you're concerned about her."

"Chief, Jacqueline is the only friend I have. If she needs me, I can't do anything but return the favor."

"Well, I have a few questions to ask you."

"Okay, shoot."

"Do you know Jacqueline's husband?"

"Actually, I've never met him. Jacqueline and I only work together and I call her on the cell phone when I need her. She's never brought him to any of the school functions because he's always working."

"Well, do you know where he works?" Chief Jones asked her, kind of feeling like the woman wasn't aware at all that she's been seeing Jacqueline's husband.

"No, I heard that he owned a car dealership. I had no need to go get a car because mine was a gift."

"So you don't say."

"Yes, I do say. A guy I mess with gave it to me."

"Can you tell me what this guy's name is?"

"Yes, his name is Big L. Well, at least that's what they call him at the club. I haven't known him long but he's been good to me so far."

"I have some pictures, can you pick Big L out if you saw a picture."

"Yes, I can."

"Okay, here are some pictures." And Chief Jones laid out four pictures of four different men. Yolanda knew Big L right away and she picked the picture of him up. "This is Big L right here." Sure enough, it was Raphiel Vance. Chief Jones knew that the woman had no idea she was, in fact, messing around with her only friend's husband. He also knew she didn't have a clue the man was dead.

"Ms. Clark, wait right here and I'll be back shortly," he said before leaving to go speak with Lieutenant Collins.

"Lieutenant, can you believe this? This girl has no clue Raphiel is Jacqueline's husband."

"Chief, I see. How could a woman get this involved with a man and know nothing about him?"

"It happens every day, Lieutenant. These women want someone to even act like they love them and they're gone. Man, I pray my twins understand that if a man becomes involved with them, I'm going to check his background right off."

"I know, man. I tried to warn Jacqueline but you have to let them make their own mistakes. She was a grown woman and I couldn't stop her from dating him. Now, this fool was messing with her friend and she didn't even know it."

"What else do I say? I got to tell this woman that he's dead and her gun was at the scene."

"I know, Chief. It's hard and who knows how she's going to react."

SHAYLA

School was finally out and Shayla dreaded walking out of the school's front doors. She knew that her worst nightmare was waiting for her outside. After most of the students had left she walked past the office doors.

"Come here, Shayla." And her heart skipped a beat. She turned and there was Mr. Brandon beckoning for her.

"Hey Mr. Brandon, what did I do now?" She was more than relieved that it was only Mr. Brandon and not the devil she'd dealt with because of her mother.

"I wanted to tell you that I am proud of you. Mr. Jacobs said that you were on your best behavior, and I thank you."

"You told me to be nice, so I did."

"Well, I see you've missed the bus. I can take you home if you don't have a way. Wait until Mrs. Brandon comes down from her classroom."

"Okay, but I'm not going home. I have to work at the shelter today so can you take me there."

"Yes, we can."

Shayla didn't know whether to jump or shout. Now she didn't even have to see what was lurking on the other side of the doors. She'd been praying all seventh hour that the Lord would provide a way of escape.

When she, Mr. and Mrs. Brandon walked out of the door, she saw the black car leaving campus.

She figured he thought she didn't come to school. Tired of cleaning his house and getting prostituted to his friends, a sigh of relief escaped her lips. Tired of getting beat up. Tired of feeling helpless. The only way she could get help was to tell somebody but she also knew her predator would stop at nothing but her death.

"Why are you such a quiet mouse, young lady?" Mrs. Brandon asked as they rode down Hearne Avenue.

"Oh, no reason, Mrs. Brandon. I'm listening to the church music y'all playing," Shayla answered.

"Do you go to church?" Mr. Brandon asked, already feeling like the answer was no.

"No, sir, my mama never took me to church. She said that Jesus ain't in the church. She didn't want to go and that was her excuse not to take me."

Ronald Brandon nodded his head because he knew now that the young lady was smarter than he thought she was. She'd answered the reasoning of her mother not taking her like he would have.

"Well, whenever you want to go, call me and I'll pick you up." Mrs. Brandon said, turning and showering Shayla with a wide bright smile.

"Yes, ma'am," she answered, returning the gesture.

"Girl, you have a beautiful smile, Shayla. Do you know that I've never seen you smile, young lady?"

"Mrs. Brandon, I don't smile because I've never had anything to smile about. I'm glad that you got a chance to see me smile."

JACQUELINE

Jacqueline decided to take a walk around the grounds armed with a can of mace that Officer Jones had given her. She needed to clear her mind and as she walked, she sang "Call Jesus" by Bruce Parham. She had no other person to call during times like these. As she sang she remembered the happy times in her life. Then she thought about her students. She thought about how they go through so much at such a young age. With that thought alone, she realized that she had nothing to be complaining about.

"God gives and God takes away, blessed be the name of the Lord," she mumbled.

Then she thought about Shayla Smith. She wondered if things had gone all right with her and Patrice. Patrice was a smart young lady. And if anyone could get through to Shayla, Patrice would be a great source of help. Then she thought about Clarence Hines. Although he was being taught about street life, he was still eager to learn from her. These two students were most of the teachers at Yorkwood headaches. But not Jacqueline. She loved both of these students like her very own children.

Before she could even finish that thought, there was little Denisia on her mind. She thought about her, a little girl who'd never know her mother. She had to admit that her dad and the baby sitter were doing an excellent job at raising her.

She wondered if they'd tried to call her. Then she made a mental note to get in contact with them and let them know that she was out of town for a while. They would have found whom they needed to find and she'd be back at Yorkwood before the end of the week.

She always loved coming out to the ranch home in Gloster when she was a little girl. Hardly anyone knew they owned the home except for policemen. Most of them came out every holiday to celebrate with barbecue and beer. Now, she still loved the atmosphere but she longed to be doing what she loved the most, teaching.

It seemed whenever things were crazy in her life, teaching the children kept her grounded. Knowing that some of them were going through the worst things always made her feel blessed. No matter what was happening in her life.

Once she finished her walk, Jacqueline went into the house. She was kind of concerned that her father hadn't returned, but she didn't want to question her mother. She fixed herself a ham sandwich, took a pickle out of the pickle jar, and grabbed a bag of potato chips. It was rare that she munched on stuff like this but today she felt like munching. She'd been eating small increments but now things were about to change. She wasn't going to mourn as a woman with no hope, but instead, she was rejoicing for the time she had with Raphiel.

Cheryl and Geraldine were watching the soaps. Neither wanted to get behind on the details. They could both watch television at their jobs. Cheryl retired from teaching, and opened a recreation center. It was for the inner city youth of Shreveport. She sat in her office doing whatever she wanted until after three o'clock. When the children and teens came in to play basketball or video games she was up and alert.

Jacqueline decided not to bother them and disappeared to her room to use the phone. She didn't need Cheryl asking questions about who she was calling.

YOLANDA

Chief Jones went back into the interrogation room where he'd left Yolanda. He was getting ready to drop a bomb on her and he knew it. She needed to know everything. She was the one with the clues to solve this murder whether she knew it or not.

"I apologize for keeping you waiting, Ms. Clark."

"Chief, it is okay. Officer James brought me in some cookies and some coffee. I need to know what Big L has to do with this and me."

"Well, I am going to share some things with you but first, I need to ask you a couple more questions."

"Okay, shoot."

"Do you know where Jacqueline Vance lives?"

"No, I've never visited her at home and she's never been to my house. I know you might think our relationship is strange but we like it this way. Jacqueline and I went to college together and she helped me through some rough times. Jacqueline preaches to me a lot about Jesus so I decided that seeing her at school was enough. You don't know how dogmatic she is about Jesus. She doesn't push Him down my throat. If I ask her a question or have a problem, the solution always ends up being about my lack of relations with Jesus. Don't get me wrong, I love that girl."

"I see. Tell me this; do you even know her husband's name?"

"Yes, his name is Raphiel Vance."

"Did you attend their wedding?"

"Actually she didn't have one. Mr. Collins was dead set against her marrying this guy and they eloped. I was away when this happened."

"Where were you?"

"I spent some time in Milledgeville, Georgia with my father who I didn't meet until I was grown. I was the product of a one night stand and from what I gathered from my mother, he didn't want any children. I guess that's why I'm so bitter with men. On that trip, he confirmed what my mother said. When I came back, Mrs. Collins told me that Jacqueline was away on her honeymoon. It shocked me because she never told me about Raphiel."

"You weren't even curious about him after that?"

"Why should I have been? As much as Jacqueline prays, if she ended up with the wrong guy, God must have been showing her something. I didn't have any reason to hunt them down or see him. And if Mr. Collins didn't like the guy, I wouldn't have either. Mr. Collins has a strong sense of judgment and he knows a crook when he sees one."

"Yolanda, do you own a gun?"

"Yes, I do. I keep it for protection. Some thugs moved down the walkway from me and I don't feel safe anymore."

"Where were you on Saturday night?"

"I slept all day Saturday. Big L stayed at my house kind of late Friday night. Well, after he'd brought me some lunch and stayed a little while I was restless when he left. I got dressed around nine and went to Adam's House. You know the bar downtown. When I got there, I noticed that Big L was there. I sent him over a couple of drinks and then he came home with me."

"Did you notice anything different around your house?"

"Those thugs were out in their usual place. Nothing but..."

"But what, Yolanda?"

"My door wasn't locked. I figured that I was rushing to get out of there so fast until I failed to lock my door."

"Have you ever forgotten to lock your door?"

"Once or twice; nothing is ever missing when I get back though."

"Did you check for your gun?"

"No, I didn't. My gun is under my mattress and no one knows it's there."

"Did Big L check your gun for you lately?"

"Yes, he put some bullets in it for me. I usually don't have any bullets in it and he said I at least needed three; in case someone did come in."

"That explains a lot."

"Chief Jones, what does all this have to do with anything?"

"Yolanda, the man you know as Big L is dead. Someone shot him on Sunday."

"No! You are lying to me. It can't be," she screamed.

"Yes, Yolanda, but that's not all. We found your gun at the scene of the crime. It had your fingerprints on it and the man you called Big L."

"Do you all think I did it? I was falling in love with him. I wouldn't have killed him. Oh God! No!" And she sobbed.

"Yolanda, that's not all, the man you call Big L is Raphiel Vance. You were having an affair with your friend's husband."

Yolanda looked at Chief Jones with a blank stare. There was no way that she was hearing what he was telling her. *There was no way that Big L was married. Not to mention married to Jacqueline.* He was with her all times of the night. Jacqueline never told her that her husband wasn't coming home at night. Then she heard a familiar voice calling her name.

"Yolanda, Yolanda, you have to talk," Hubert Collins said as he shook her shoulder.

"Oh, Mr. Collins, I wouldn't have ever done that to Jacqueline. I didn't know. I didn't know."

"I know you didn't, Yolanda. Come on, baby. You've got to pull it together. You can help solve this murder but you've got to pull it together."

"Oh my goodness, does Jacqueline know I betrayed her? She'll never forgive me, Mr. Collins. She would have never done this to me."

"No, she doesn't know. She knows that he was cheating but with whom she doesn't have a clue. Raphiel knew exactly who you were though."

"Come to think of it, the night he met me, he already knew my name. He walked over to me and he called out my name. I asked him how he knew me and he said that the bartender had told him. I should have known that he was too good to be true. He never wore a wedding ring and he never acted like a married man."

"I know, Yolanda. We know he cheated with you to get back at Jacqueline. He was so upset that she'd decided to change her life. This was the only way he could hurt her. By sleeping with you, if she found out, she'd quit her job and that's exactly what he wanted. He was jealous of her job."

"Oh my goodness, she's going to hate me."

"No, because if I have my way, she'll never know that it was you. He's dead now and there's no reason for her to know who you were."

BRADLEY

Bradley drove back to his home in hopes that Jacqueline would call him. He wanted to know if she was okay. Like him, Denisia must have had her on her mind. Before he dropped her off at Mrs. Burch house, she asked him to call her.

Somehow, this woman had changed their lives in a few hours. He walked in and went straight to his caller id. After he searched his calls, he went to retrieve her card from his phone book. His thoughts were interrupted when he heard the phone ring. Without checking the caller id, he answered.

"Hi, Bradley," Jacqueline said, sounding almost as if she were about to cry. "I was hoping that you were home."

"Hey, Jacqueline, how are you? Is everything okay?"

"Slow down. I'm fine, well blessed I should say and all is well. I don't know if you saw it or not but that was my husband who was murdered on Sunday. I put him out on Saturday and he returned home to get some things. It's been an ordeal, but I know that God is working things out."

"I saw. I knew the address from your business card. I'm so sorry that you're going through this right now. I know how it is to lose a spouse.

And you're right. God will work it out. You have to know that it's all in His divine plan."

"Bradley, I know but every now and then my heart aches."

"Tell me about it. I know. It's been three years and sometimes it feel like it was yesterday. Through it all, I thank God that I have Denisia. Without her, Jacqueline, I don't know what I would have done."

"Well, I'm grateful for my parents and his aunt Geraldine. They've been helping me stay grounded. Due to the fact they don't know who murdered him, I'm in hiding, and will be here for a while."

"So I guess we won't be seeing you at the theater on Saturday."

"Unfortunately, I won't be there. I wish this was all over but I guess in due time God will reveal things."

"Yes, He will. You remember there is no sorrow, heaven can't heal. We go through to get over; over the level we were, unto the next level where we need to be."

"Thank you for the encouragement, Bradley. Look, tell Denisia I said hello and as soon as all this is over, I'll meet you guys at the movies."

"Okay, Jacqueline and I'll keep praying for you." And they both hung up the phone.

SHAYLA

Mr. Brandon looked back at Shayla. "All right, looks like we're here."

"Thank you, Mr. Brandon, and you too, Mrs. Brandon."

"You're welcome, young lady. Anytime you miss the bus, come to my classroom and you can ride with us," Mrs. Brandon said.

Wow, God is doing what Mrs. Vance says He would. Work things out. "Bye."

"Have a blessed day, Shayla," Mr. Brandon said before pulling off.

Shayla was about to open the shelter door when she felt something poking her in her side.

"You thought you were smart, didn't you? Your mother owes me and you are going to do whatever I say until I'm paid in full."

"Please leave me alone! I'm tired of doing things for your friends. I want to go to school."

"Look here, I'm not stopping you from going to school but I will stop you from living. You better not play with me or you'll end up in the news like that Vance man."

"What did you say?"

"You heard me. Get your crap and let's go." And she followed him to his car and got in.

Shayla never watched the news because it was for old folks. Anyway, all they showed was black people in the ghetto committing crimes. They never showed the white folks who were doing bad things. Still, she needed to find out about the Vance man. Could it be Mrs. Vance's husband he was talking about? She was absent from school today and no one knew when she was coming back.

"If he did anything to Mrs. Vance, I'll kill him myself," she thought. Mrs. Vance was all she had and she was the only person who believed in her. She was quiet the whole ride but in her mind, she was planning her escape. She wasn't about to sleep with anyone else she didn't want too. It was her mother who needed the drugs and not her. If she was going to continue to run to him for the drugs, she had to pay for them with her own body. After today, Shayla made it up in her mind that she wouldn't be the one who suffered for her mother's high.

YOLANDA

"Yolanda, tell me this...did Raphiel talk about any of his clients who didn't like him or anyone who he'd upset?" Hubert asked.

"No, he never talked about much of anything. He always said he needed me. He told me that I was a part of his escape plan."

"Did he say what he was escaping from?"

"No, Mr. Collins, he never said. I felt needed whenever he was around. I even told Jacqueline that I thought I'd found the one; the one man who loved me for me. Now I see that even that was a lie."

"Yolanda, you are a beautiful young lady. Women don't find men but men find the woman they respect enough to be their wife. For a man who loves God to find you, you must be in the right position. I know you're wondering where the right position is. The right position is where men who love God are at."

"You know Jacqueline always says that. But every time I go to church, I always run into some married man who wants a mistress."

"See, that's exactly what you were trying to avoid but look at where you still ended up with that same kind of man. Yolanda, the church is a hospital and people are sin sick but want healing. Everybody that goes to church isn't saved. Some folks go because their parents went. But then, there are those in the church who love the Lord. They've made a conscious decision to live and love right. You still stand a better chance at church getting a man who is sick but on the verge of his healing. Now don't get me wrong, you may go to a church for thirty years and never get a husband. But get this; the church is not the building, the church is the one who believes. He might find you in the grocery store or at a picnic. So all I can say is now you must get your heart right."

"Yes, sir, all I know is that I'd never ever want to hurt Jacqueline. I know that somehow this news will come out and I don't want her finding out from some news reporter. I don't want her to know at all but if she must, I'd prefer it to come from me. I'm willing to take whatever my fate is."

"I'm happy to hear you say that. Now I know that you love my daughter. Yolanda, I always wondered why she was your friend but now I see. God linked the two of you so that you could see how mighty He is."

"Chief Jones, what is going to happen now?"

"First, we are going to take you out to where Jacqueline is so that you two can talk. Whoever did this is going to be expecting you to be picked up and charged. They wanted to frame you for this murder. Once they believe that you've gotten charged with the murder, they'll mess up in some kind of way. Murderers always find a way to tell off on themselves. With the help of the evening news, they'll think we have you in custody. We are going to set up a surveillance crew by your apartment and watch who is coming and going."

"Will everyone know it's me?"

"We are going to try to keep your name out of the media. Whoever it is might try to kill you too."

"Oh no!"

"This is serious, Ms. Clark. We are going to do whatever possible to keep you safe. In the meantime, if you can think of anything else, tell Lieutenant Collins."

"All right, I sure will." Then Hubert Collins led her to a black tinted windowed detective car and they both got in.

BRADLEY

Bradley couldn't believe that Jacqueline called him. He'd hope that his words of encouragement help. She was a wise and kind woman and these things shouldn't have been happening to her. He wished there was a way he could wash away the sadness in her voice. He'd experienced first-hand how the heart tends to be heavy even when the mind feels light. So he decided to do what he knew was best to do for her; he whispered a word of prayer on her behalf.

Afterward, he sat down in his rocker and turned on the news. He started to call the store but decided against it. There was no way he wanted Michelle to think he thought she was incapable of handling things. She was his rock when it came to Tequila Delights and she could handle things as good as he could. He decided to catch the news to see if they'd found out anything about the murder of Jacqueline's husband. He'd been watching for over twenty minutes and they hadn't said anything.

Bradley put his shoes on and decided to go get Denisia early. He was beginning to miss her. Usually, when he took off, it was so that they could be together. Today he needed some alone time with the Lord and he'd been able to get that. He was so thankful for Mrs. Burch. She was indeed worthy of all the praise he could give her. Not only for ensuring that Denisia was well taken care of, but for allowing him the alone time he needed.

JACQUELINE

Jacqueline laid across her bed thinking about Bradley and Denisia. She'd thought of them often since their chance meeting at the theater. Unfortunately, she could never consider things going any further between them. Raphiel thought she was already seeing Bradley. Making the decision to become involved with him would only make her feel guilty. Jacqueline sat up and rebuked the devil.

There should have been nothing on her mind about another man. She should have been still weeping. But if she would be honest with everyone including herself, her marriage to Raphiel was over a long time ago. Jacqueline hung so hard to the dream of a wonderful marriage to Raphiel for so long. Two months after her second miscarriage, things got worse. Raphiel made it clear that they will never be happy without a child. Her mind couldn't help but drift to the day when things changed forever.

"Mrs. Vance, I am so sorry to inform you that your child is stillborn," Dr. Razpa said, holding on to her hand for comfort.

"You mean to tell me that my baby is dead," Raphiel said with an immense tensed look of anger in his eyes.

"Yes, Raphiel, we are going to do a DNC on Jacqueline and I am going to ask you to take care of her these next few days."

"Dr. Razpa, she didn't take care of herself so that our baby could live, so I won't be taking care of her."

"Mr. Vance, it's not her fault that the baby is stillborn. We sometimes never find the reason why. I'm going to leave the two of you alone so you can talk. Jacqueline, I'll be praying for you," Dr. Razpa said before he left the room.

"I don't care what he said; You never wanted the baby in the first place."

"Raphiel, why are you trying to hurt me? I loved this baby as much as you. Do you think I'm happy this happened?"

"I don't know, Jacqueline. Until you are pregnant with my child, things won't change. And until I hold my baby in my arms, I'll never be responsible for making you happy again." Raphiel said before leaving her all alone.

Jacqueline began to cry at the thought of that awful day. She had never felt so alone and betrayed in her entire life.

A small part of her wished she would have died instead of the baby. It was clear that Raphiel forgot about the part of the vow he made. *To love, honor, and respect in good times and in bad.* He was so consumed with what he wanted until nothing else mattered to him; not even her. The next couple of months following that horrible day were even worse.

Things were crazy whenever they received pictures from friends. Pictures of their family portraits with children or a new baby. He even began to despise the relationship she had with her students. She kept praying God would change Raphiel's heart and His mind toward giving them a child.

None of that mattered now. Raphiel was gone and she didn't even get a chance to tell him that she loved him in spite of how he treated her. Jacqueline's thoughts broke when she heard someone coming through the front door.

SHAYLA

Shayla stood at the door trying to hear what the men in the other room were saying. All she could make out was a couple of words here and there.

"I   murdered.....rich   guy.........Vance's   Dealership..........police...........that trick.......B24_........."

The harder she tried to listen, the lower their voices became. She'd heard him earlier when he made mention to the Vance man and she wondered then if it was Mrs. Vance's husband. As soon as she heard the word dealership, she knew that's who it was. Mrs. Vance always talked about how her husband owned a car dealership. She used their ability to save money to teach her class that they could save enough money to do whatever they wanted too.

Shayla remained as quiet as a mouse in hopes that she would hear something else and then the door slammed. Then she heard the two men outside in what seemed to have been a heated argument. They were cussing each other out and threatening to shoot one another. She tiptoed to the window so she could peek out. All she saw was a blue sports car.

She realized she could make out the license plate number. She said the number, XRT 143, over and over again in her head. She needed to remember that number like her life depended on it. Then she heard the front door slam. She hurried away from the window and made her way to the center of the room. She picked up the broom and started back sweeping. If he would have caught her being noisy, she knew he would have beaten her alive.

"Are you finished?"

"I'm almost done," Shayla yelled and then swallowed real hard, as she released a breath of air.

"Hurry up! I got some business to handle."

"Okay," she said.

"Lord, please. I know you are real and that you love Mrs. Vance. Please let me get to her so I can give her this news. I know he killed her husband and I know he would kill me if I made the wrong move. Please give me the strength and the courage to do what I have to do. And Lord, keep your arms of protection around Mrs. Vance. Remember when she told me that I was not too far gone for You to love me and for You to change my life. Well, please love me enough to get me out of this and then change my life."

As Shayla was about to open the door, she heard some gunshots. She'd never heard that sound before except for on television. It sounded like a machine gun.

Shayla jumped under the bed and covered her ears with her hands. Then things were quiet. She was too afraid to leave the room. She'd watched a lot of the detective shows on television with this sort of thing happening. She decided to stay put for at least another thirty minutes and then she'd make a run for it.

Mr. Ratman was waiting for Shayla to come in from school. She had been a blessing to him and the others at the shelter since she'd been there. Although she started out as a mean child filled with hatred, her heart was being changed.

She wasn't the hard-hearted, distant child that she was from the beginning. She was helpful. She had even got some of the other children to take part in the after-school tutoring classes. His mind went back to the punk who was trying to take her out of the shelter a few days ago. He didn't know whether to call the police or what.

He'd tried locating a couple of the officer friends but he couldn't reach any of them. Then, he went to her mother who was alert to ask her if she knew where she could be. Like he thought, she was no help. He wondered if she even knew where she was.

One of the rules of staying at the shelter was that you had to be drug-free. Mr. Ratman had allowed them to stay only because of Shayla. He'd felt sorry for the little girl who instead of being a teenager, was a mother to her own mother. He'd given them a permanent room at the shelter with conditions. As long as Shayla went to school, stayed out of trouble, and helped him around the shelter they could stay. He wasn't sure why God pricked his heart about the girl but now that He had, he worried about her.

Mr. Ratman decided to drive around the city looking for her. He drove in the direction of Pete Street. The spot for the local gangs and drug-addicted folks in the city. As he drove he noticed a blue car speeding by as if they were running from the cops. He was so happy that he didn't decide to turn because if he had, that car would have torn his car to pieces. When he reached the corner of Pete, there was a strong urging from the Holy Spirit for him to pray. Mr. Ratman pulled over because he knew that when the Lord spoke, he had nothing better to do than to listen and obey.

"Father, I don't know where Shayla is or what is going on with her. Lord, you said in your word that no weapon formed against us will prosper. She is your child too. Whatever weapon that has formed against her this day, Lord don't let it prosper. I claim the victory for her life, Lord. Satan is defeated in the name of Jesus. Satan the Lord rebukes you now about this child, in Jesus's name. Amen."

JACQUELINE & YOLANDA

"Hey, Yolanda, what are you doing here? Did Dad bring you here to see me?"

"Hey, Jacqueline, I'm here because we need to talk."

"Why are you sounding so serious? Girl, what is going on?"

"Jacqueline, I have something to tell you."

"I thought I heard you come in, Hubert. Hey, Yolanda, how are you?" Cheryl said, looking at her husband with a million questions in her eyes.

"I'm fine, Mrs. Collins," Yolanda said and lowered her head.

"Yes, I'm back, baby. Look, Yolanda needs to talk to Jacqueline. Why don't you, Geraldine, and I go out back for a little while?" Hubert said.

"I know you. Aren't you Big L's aunt or something?" Yolanda asked, looking at Geraldine, causing her to drop her head in shame.

"Yes, I am Raphiel's aunt, but I don't remember you,"

Geraldine said, trying to brush the young woman off and exit the room.

"Okay. It was nice seeing you again, Yolanda," Cheryl said.

"You, too, Mrs. Collins," Yolanda said before Collins and Geraldine went out back.

"Jacqueline."

"Yes," Jacqueline answered.

"Do you remember me telling you about the guy I called my Mr. Do Me Right?"

"Yes, what about him, Yolanda?"

"I found out his real name today. All I ever heard the guys at the bar calling him is Big L. I planned on finding out more about him when he came back to my house. He never came."

"Okay, Yolanda. What does any of this have to do with me?"

"Jacqueline, he was your husband."

"What!"

"I'm so sorry. I would have never done that to you," Yolanda pleaded.

"You mean to tell me that you were the one sleeping with Raphiel. All those stories about Mr. Do You Right; all the time you were talking about my husband."

"Jacqueline, I'm so sorry."

"Get out! Get out now!"

"But, Jacqueline, I promise you I didn't know. Now someone is trying to frame me for his murder. Jacqueline, I loved him too. I was falling in love with him. He told me that he was going to be moving in with me. I didn't know."

"Now you know! I've told you over and over again about sleeping around with everyone and you never listened. That's the very reason why I never brought you to my house. I couldn't trust you and you still found a way to sleep with my husband."

"Jacqueline, you are all I have. When my mom died, you promised you'd never leave me. I'm sorry, Jacqueline." And Yolanda fell to her knees crying with her face buried in shame. Jacqueline didn't know what to think. She was still in shock. How could this be? Her husband was sleeping with her friend. Jacqueline stormed out of the room, leaving Yolanda there crying her eyes out. She ran in her room and slammed the door.

It took Jacqueline a while to collect herself. When she was able to face the situation at hand, she came back to the room where Yolanda waited.

How long has this been going on? Jacqueline asked herself, still feeling like she was in a daze. "All those times she was talking about my husband," she mumbled. Then she laid on her bed, clutched her pillow, balled up in a knot, and cried.

As Jacqueline laid almost still in disbelief, she thought about what Yolanda said. She never took Yolanda to meet Raphiel. In all these years, some part of her was afraid that he'd find her attractive. He'd long stopped husband duties with her in their bedroom so she figured he was with someone else. Never in a million years would she have thought that it was Yolanda.

※

Hubert explained to Cheryl and Geraldine what was going on with Yolanda. Both of the women were in absolute shock. Geraldine wouldn't have ever thought that Raphiel would be so vindictive. She knew for a fact that Raphiel knew exactly who Yolanda was. Guilt made her decide not to say anything, but she felt so much remorse for Jacqueline. She remembered the day that Yolanda came into the restaurant.

"Hi, pretty lady," Raphiel said, ignoring Geraldine's blatant stare in his direction.

"Hi," Yolanda said and then she switched to her table across from theirs.

"You look like a businesswoman. Do you work at a bank or something?"

"No, I work at Yorkwood High."

"They call me Big L," he said with a smirk across his face.

Geraldine thought she should have been off limits. Especially since she worked at the same place as Jacqueline. Instead, it seemed that she was the ammunition. He needed to get back at Jacqueline and he pursued her. Geraldine felt so ashamed that she had even been his aunt. He had no right to hurt Jacqueline the way he had and even now, he was still tearing her apart.

"I tried to warn him, Cheryl. I pleaded with Raphiel not to cheat on Jacqueline. He told me to mind my own business. After I didn't see her in the office, I figured that he had taken my advice. I'm so sorry."

"Geraldine, Raphiel was a grown man and he made his own bed and now he's lying in it. We don't hold anything against you. You are still a part of my daughter and she still loves you."

"You don't know how much I told that boy that he was wrong. I told him that the same ditch you dig would be the one you fell in. He fell and he fell hard. I didn't realize that Raphiel needed help."

"He needed more than help," Hubert said as he looked at the ladies.

"Hubert, now Hubert! The boy lost both his parents and no one ever counseled him." Cheryl said, knowing all too well Hubert had to respect the love Geraldine had for the man. He had become her only child. She continued speaking. "Then when Jacqueline lost both of those babies, it blew him away. He wanted to hurt someone for all the hurt he suffered." Cheryl said, all the while hoping her husband would stop the negative talk.

"I pray the Lord has mercy on him and his soul," Hubert said, still feeling like he got what he deserved. It was harsh, but Hubert believed in reaping what you sowed. And all Raphiel sowed was what he had reaped.

"Me too," Cheryl said, for the first time not knowing if her husband Hubert meant what he said.

"I know I raised him the best I could. When my sister and her husband died, I took the boy as my very own. I did all I could. But he was too hotheaded," Geraldine mumbled through tears that seemed to freeze on her cheeks. "If he wanted to do something, nothing or no one could stop him. I need to go and talk to Jacqueline. Is it okay with you all?"

"It is, Geraldine," Cheryl answered.

SHAYLA

Sharon Smith was high but she wasn't too high to grasp that her only daughter was missing. She pulled on her shoes and started walking in the direction of Pete Street. She knew exactly where her baby was. She'd been having Shayla pay her debt to T J since she was ten years old. Shayla was the only way T J would deal with her or give her any of his products. She was still kind of in her high zone but she saw the car coming toward her.

As her eyes blurred, and she finally began to focus she saw the car only inches away. She could do nothing. Her reflexes were so slow until she couldn't even jump out of the way if she wanted to. And then, BOOM! Her body flew into the air like a rag and landed on the street.

"Sharon, Sharon, oh Lord have mercy?" Mr. Ratman yelled as he jumped out of his car and ran toward the woman. "Do you know those men?"

"Yes, she said with a slur. It was those Hines boys. Ratman, please tell Shayla that I'm sorry. I love her. Lord, please forgive me." And she closed her eyes. Mr. Ratman stayed by Sharon's side, calling her name over and over. It seemed like forever when the paramedics arrived. They told Mr. Ratman they were taking Sharon to Louisiana Day Hospital.

As the ambulance drove away with Sharon, Mr. Ratman did his best to describe the blue car that ran Sharon over. He was hysterical having watched the accident and hurt that he hadn't been there in time to save her. He told the officers about the incident that happened between him and T. J.

He also had already reported Shayla was missing. Mr. Ratman had known Sharon's habit cost her much more than she'd ever thought it would. After the officers finished their line of questioning, he went back to his car, and sat there.

Shayla came from under the bed. Then she went to the window to see if any cars were still in front of the house. All she saw was T. J.'s car but there was no sign of him. She opened the bedroom door real slow. T. J. laid on the floor covered in blood. Shayla swallowed hard and put her hands over her eyes as she slid by the body.

She took a shirt that was lying on the back of a chair and turned the knob. Once she was out of the door, Shayla ran so fast that it was hard for her to even catch her breath. She would not stop running until she'd made it to the shelter. When she turned the corner from Pete Street onto Milam Street, she saw a familiar car. Then she noticed it was Mr. Ratman. With every piece of strength she had, she hollered, "HELP ME!"

Mr. Ratman looked into his rearview mirror. He'd heard the distant cry for help but didn't know where it was coming from. As soon as he turned his head, there was a poor, worn out child, running toward his car. He jumped out because at first glance he recognized her.

"Shayla, sweet child, where have you been?"

"Oh, Mr. Ratman," she cried and then fell into his arms, exhausted and tired.

Mr. Ratman took out his cell phone and called 911. He didn't want to take her from the spot where she'd found him. He knew what happened to her was beyond him. The child looked like she'd been in a hot box or somewhere with no air. Mr. Ratman picked the child up and put her in his car. As soon as the police arrived, they had Ratman take Shayla to Louisiana Day for an examination.

JACQUELINE

Knock. Knock.

"Who is it?"

"It's Geraldine."

"Come in," Jacqueline said but in heart she wanted her to go away. Not that she'd done anything wrong but she wasn't in the mood to talk about anything.

"Jacqueline, sweetheart, I am so sorry that Raphiel has hurt you as he has. Still, no matter what someone has done, you are still who you are. You are born again, fire baptized Christian and as a Christian, you must walk in forgiveness. Now, you can tell me to get out but you know that I am telling the truth. I know that Raphiel was my nephew but that doesn't excuse him for the evilness in his heart. He never got over the fact that the baby died. He blamed you, Jacqueline, and sleeping with Yolanda was his way of getting back at you. I was there when he met her and he knew exactly where she worked. I told him to leave that child alone, but he didn't listen. You deserved better Jacqueline and now the Lord has seen fit for you to start over. Do you think Raphiel thought he was getting ready to die?"

"No, ma'am…"

"See, if he knew, he would have gotten himself together. Baby, see sometimes we get too far out there to turn around. God is beckoning for us with each breath to give our lives to Him. Whether we choose to do so is all up to us. Raphiel chose to do it his way and when you live by the sword, you die by the sword."

"I can't believe that he would try to hurt me like this."

"When a man isn't saved, Jacqueline, there's no telling what he would or wouldn't do. I can't put Raphiel in hell but I shole can't put him in heaven. Whether he believed it or not, I couldn't tell. All I know is that he didn't live like a saved man. He put his trust in his riches and not in the Lord. Now he's gone and his money couldn't keep him. Now you have a friend who is downstairs still crying her eyes out. She is at the point of breakdown and the only one who can save her is Jesus. Even so, who will offer Jesus to her? You are in a position to show Yolanda how saved folks love, live, and forgive."

"I don't know, Aunt Geraldine."

"What don't you know? It is what it is. If we want God to forgive us our trespasses, we sure have to forgive others theirs."

"I know you're right, Aunt Geraldine, but."

"But what, Jacqueline? Look, child, don't let the devil steal what God has in store for you. He didn't bring you this far for you to go second guessing Him. We are going to bury Raphiel and you are going to move on. God has a bigger plan in store for you."

"How do I forget?"

"Sometimes you never forget, but forgiving causes you to sleep easy."

"Okay, Auntie, I understand."

"You do, darling. I love you, Jacqueline, and I always will."

"I love you too, Auntie. I'll never stop loving you either."

"I want you to know, whoever you marry in the future, they better know that I belong in the family too."

"They will if it ever happens."

SHAYLA

"Shayla, my name is Chief Jones; can you tell me what happened to you today?"

"Yes, sir, Mr. and Mrs. Brandon dropped me off at the shelter. I was about to go in when T. J. put a pistol to my side and told me to come with him. I couldn't scream because he would have killed me. He told me that I'd be like the Mr. Vance man. I didn't know what happened to Mr. Vance but with T. J., I knew it couldn't have been good."

"What else happened?"

"He made me go to the drug house on Pete Street. He threw me in the room and told me to clean it up. While I was there, I heard him and someone arguing about the murder. I struggled but I did hear them say, "Rich guy, Vance's dealership, killed, that trick, and B24.""

"Okay did they say anything else?"

"They kept arguing but they were getting further away so it was harder for me to hear. Then I went over to the window. I saw a blue car and I memorized the license plate number. It was X...RT...1...4........3. I kept saying it but when I heard the gunshots, I forgot everything. I jumped under the bed and tried to be as quiet as I could."

"Someone ran that plate number," Chief Jones instructed the officer who was in the room with them. "So then what happened?"

"I stayed there and started praying. After about what seemed to be an hour, I got up. I opened the door and T J was lying in a puddle of blood. I eased by and I started running. I ran. Then when I saw Mr. Ratman's car, I knew God didn't forget about me. I ran until I got there."

"Okay, darling, it's going to be fine. You wait here with Mr. Ratman and the doctor is going to check you out. I'm going to put two policemen by this door to make sure that no one gets in here to harm you."

"Yes, sir, Chief Jones. Thank you."

"You are welcome, baby. Thank you for being such a smart girl and getting the number on that car." And Chief Jones left the room.

"Hey, Lieutenant, you'll never believe what happened!"

"What, Chief? Is it more drama than the drama I have going on here with these women."

"Yeah, that's right you do have your hands full."

"Sure do, but what's going on?"

"How about we got a teenager who T J Hines kidnaped. She overheard him and someone arguing about the murder of the car dealer. She struggled to make out what they were saying but she did get some keywords. We were able to fit the puzzle together. You know that his sister works for apartment management. She got keys to Yolanda's house and they broke in and took her gun. I've had her, the other brother, and the nephews picked up for questioning."

"Man, this family has been a headache to this department for years. Do you think we finally have enough evidence to do something?"

"Well, looks like we don't have T J to worry about. He was murdered this afternoon. And the plates the teenager remembered came back as registered to Terry Hines."

"Do you think he killed his own brother, Chief?"

"Yeah, Lieutenant, the heat was getting too hot. When he murdered Raphiel, they had to knock him off."

"Yes, because it was crackheads and drug dealers they killed. Now he was going too far for them."

"I hope things turn out and in the meantime, I'm going to let Jacqueline know what's going on."

"Okay, Lieutenant. I'll call you if I get anything else."

"All right, son, thanks a lot."

Hubert felt relieved that they finally had some sort of lead about who killed Raphiel. He would have never been able to sleep at night knowing that his child was in danger. Why didn't she marry a man like Carlos Jones? He thought after he hung up from the Chief.

He'd tried to introduce the two of them when Carlos and his lifelong girlfriend Stephanie had broken up. He thought that they might have a chance. But there was no denying that Carlos would love Stephanie forever. Now they had two twin girls and their life was wonderful. And Jacqueline married a nightmare, but thank God, that too was over.

BRADLEY

"This is Shanice Johnson with KVET News. We are at a house on Pete Street where the victim, Thomas Hines Jr. was the direct target of the shooter. Some of you may know Thomas HinesJr. as T. J. Sources say that there was never enough evidence to convict him of some of the murders attached to his name. We've also heard that this homicide connects to the murder of the owner of Vance's Dealership, Raphiel Vance.

"I'm here with Officer Jones of the Shreveport Police Department. Officer Jones, we hear that he'd kidnaped a teenager and she'd brought you to the crime scene?"

Officer Jones looked annoyed. "I'm sorry but now we have no comment on that."

"Do you have any leads? Is this homicide also linked to the murder of Raphiel Vance?"

"We're working on that right now as we speak. We're trying to unravel a puzzle."

"Thank you, Officer Jones.

"Well, you heard it. Police officers do believe they have a lead on the gunmen. Hopefully, we can get more information before the night is over. This is Shanice Johnson reporting for KVET. Back to the studio."

Bradley couldn't believe what he was hearing. He knew T J and his kind. *Was Jacqueline the wife of a drug addict or dealer?* She was an intelligent woman and he couldn't see her getting hooked up with that kind of person.

He picked up the phone to call her but decided against it. He figured that she'd call him when she was ready to talk. Bradley went to Denisia's room to check on her. She was fast asleep so he kissed her, turned off her night light, whispered a prayer for her, and then left her room.

SHAYLA

"Hey, Mr. Ratman, are you still here?"

"Yes, I am a little girl. All the women at the shelter told me to tell you hi. They also said that they were so proud of you. I heard the doctors say that they are going to keep you here for a couple of nights for observation."

Shayla stood in the doorway looking horrified. "Have you talked to my mom?"

"Shayla, there is something that I need to tell you."

Shayla could tell by the look in his eyes that whatever it was wasn't good. She felt a knot tighten in her stomach. She almost wanted to tell him not to tell her but she knew she needed to know.

"Sharon is here in critical condition. She was trying to go looking for you and she got run over by the very car that you saw at that house."

Shayla wanted the truth. No beating around the bush. She had one and only one question. "No. Is my mommy dead?"

"No, darling, she's alive. In the morning, I will take you to her. Right now I need you to get some rest."

"Do you promise, Mr. Ratman?" she said as tears flowed down her cheeks like a river rushing to meet a dam.

"Yes, baby girl, and have I ever broken a promise?" He said, drying her eyes with the tissue he'd gotten out of the hospital room cabinet.

"No, sir."

"Now you get some rest and we'll go first thing in the morning."

JACQUELINE

"Yolanda, I forgive you. I don't understand this but I know God knows."

"Jacqueline, thank you. I don't know what I would have done if you'd decided not to talk to me. I want to kill myself."

"I rebuke the spirit of suicide right now, in the name of Jesus. Suicide is not the answer. Even if I never spoke to you again, there is nothing that should make you want to kill yourself. You know, the devil tries to steal our hopes in times like these. You have to know that you know nothing is too hard for God to solve."

"How can you still be so nice to me after all I've done to you and to your family?"

"Yolanda, trust me, someone had to remind me who I was in Christ. See, it is like our civic duty to forgive. Raphiel knew exactly who you were, but you didn't know him. You were his target to get back at me. What he didn't know is that because I know a true and risen Savior, and no weapon formed against me will ever prosper. Not only that, the Word tells me that every tongue that rises up against me will get condemned. I'm still here, but Raphiel isn't."

"Jacqueline, you've always tried to get me to go to church and believe. Now, I'm ready. Tell me, how can I change?"

"Yolanda you first have to invite Jesus into your heart. If you'd like, I'll pray with you. You repeat after me."

"Okay, Jacqueline."

"Lord, Jesus, I believe with my heart that God raised you from the dead. I confess that you are a true and risen Savior. Now I ask you to forgive me for my sins. Come into my heart, Lord, and save me. In Jesus's name, amen."

"That's it," Jacqueline replied. "You are now my sister."

"That's all I have to do?" Yolanda asked.

"You are saved. Now as a symbol you can get baptized. Baptism symbolizes your old man dying and you emerging into a new creature. Like Christ was baptized. Then you ask the Lord to allow His Holy Spirit to dwell in you. Now going to church helps you to develop as a Christian. The word will mature you and you'll never want to do those old things again."

"You think?" Yolanda questioned as if it were all too easy.

"I know. That's why I don't go to the clubs or to places that I wouldn't think Jesus would like to go. I know that His Spirit lives on the inside of me and He makes me sensitive to the places I go. I don't down anyone else for going because some people are true believers and they still go to clubs. Besides, I don't want to take the Holy Spirit to a club," Jacqueline said.

"It does sound crazy, doesn't it?" Yolanda replied.

"God is in you and you take Him to the club."

"See, that's why I stopped. Even in our intellect, we'll never know God's ways or His thoughts. That might not even matter to Him, but if it does, then I want to live doing what is right. So I guess I'm saying if it doesn't align with the word of God, then it's not right."

"I understand, Jacqueline. My grandmother used to say, 'What seems right for us will lead us straight to hell.'"

"She had a point. We take the things we like and want to do and make them right because it's what we want to do. God sees and he knows and if it's shameful to us, then God is not pleased. I may sound silly. Yet, I found out if I have to hide to do something. Or if there's guilt or shame after doing something, then that was my sign that I shouldn't be doing it. As you grow in spiritual maturity, you'll be able to know the things of God. You'll learn to align your life to His Word to be the example that He would want you to be."

"Thanks, Jacqueline. I love you and I do thank you for everything."

"I love you too, Yolanda. I'm glad we are finally sisters in Christ."

Cheryl squeezed Hubert's hand as they listened to their daughter from the next room. She was all that they'd raised her to be and they had the right to be proud parents. Hubert bent down and kissed his wife on the forehead as tears peeked from her eyes.

Who would have ever thought that she'd be going through this type of situation? Even more, who would have ever known that she'd be accredited for bringing someone to Christ? Now she has. She'd, through her ability to forgive, given someone hope in the blessed Savior. Geraldine wasn't too far either.

As soon as she'd heard the ladies she ran to find Cheryl and Hubert who were already caught into the moment. They had raised a wonderful young lady and she wished that Raphiel knew what kind of lady he had. When Jaqueline and Yolanda entered the kitchen, the air froze. Everyone gathered and stared in their direction. When they smiled, the family welcomed Yolanda into their real family. and into their hearts.

CHIEF JONES

"It was me. I shot my uncle." Clarence Hines said as he broke into the conversation.

"Son, stop, don't say that." Hattie Hines screamed at her son.

"Yes, mama, I have to say it. He killed Mrs. Vance's husband and he wasn't supposed to do that. I love Mrs. Vance and he caused her pain."

"Son, is what you're saying true?" Chief Jones asked.

"Yes, sir."

"Clarence, why did you do it?" Chief Jones asked the young boy who was crying so hard.

"I saw Mr. Vance coming from Ms. Clark's house. I knew that Ms. Clark was Mrs. Vance's friend. Mr. Vance called me to his car and showed me his gun. He gave me two hundred dollars and said I better not tell anyone. I told my uncle but I didn't want him to kill Mr. Vance. When I told my uncle Terry, we went to the house where T J sells drugs. He had my sister Shayla and he wouldn't let her go. He told my uncle Terry that he would kill Mrs. Vance too if he wanted to. My uncle Terry told me not to worry about it but I dropped him off and I went back. T J pulled out his gun and shot at me and I took Uncle Terry's gun from under the seat and I shot at him. I'm sorry mama. I didn't mean to kill him but he was going to kill me."

"Clarence, how did you know that Shayla was your sister?" His mother asked.

"Because T J told me that he was going to kill my sister too. He said that you and Shayla's mother were best friends and my dad got her pregnant. He said that he got Sharon hooked on drugs so that he could use Shayla as his slave."

"Lord!" Hattie screamed out. "Baby, I didn't want you to find out like this. I didn't know my brother was so cruel."

"Yes, he was Mrs. Hines. We've been trying to get him for some murders but he always seemed to slip through the cracks."

"What are you going to do to my baby?"

"If his story pans out, and we find a gunshot in the car, we will lean toward self-defense. Still, he did run over Sharon Smith. How did that happen, Clarence?"

"I was driving so fast trying to get as far away from Pete Street as I could. I saw her and it looked like she was going to stop but then, she walked out in front of the car. I was so scared. I kept going."

"Mrs. Hines, there is where the problem will be. We could charge him with reckless operation of a vehicle but if she dies it will be vehicular homicide. Ms. Smith is in intensive care and as soon as she comes around, we can get her story about what happened. We pray she comes around. In the meantime, I am going to book Clarence in the juvenile facility until we do some work. I can assure you that he will be okay there."

"Thank you, Chief Jones."

"It's going to be all right baby," Hattie assured her child. "I am trusting and believing in the Lord."

Chief Jones couldn't wait to tell Lieutenant Collins what had transpired. He sent Clarence to a juvenile facility, cleared the reporters from his office, and put on his jacket. He could give the Collins family some good news himself.

ᔆ

Knock. Knock. Knock.

Because it was such a defining knock, Hubert decided he had better answer the door himself.

"Who is it?'

"Lieutenant, it's me, Chief."

"To what do we owe this pleasure?"

"Well, I have some news for everyone. You all had better sit down." He said motioning towards the sofa. All eyes were on him. Hubert and Cheryl sat on the love seat while Jacqueline, Yolanda, and Geraldine sat on the sofa.

"Seems like your student Clarence Hines saw Raphiel coming out of Yolanda's apartment. Raphiel gave him two hundred dollars which the boy still has and we're checking for fingerprints. He said Raphiel showed him a gun and told him that if he said anything, he'd use it. The young man told his uncle who was the neighborhood thug."

"You mean to tell me that Raphiel threatened the child?" Geraldine asked.

"Yes, ma'am, that's what the kid said and he's telling the truth. After he told the uncle, the uncle killed Raphiel. He wasn't by himself but we don't know who was with him. When the kid found out, he told his other uncle. Now the uncle who killed Raphiel was holding Clarence's sister Shayla hostage."

"Clarence and Shayla are brothers and sisters?" Jacqueline asked.

"Yes, Clarence's mother had been best friends with Shayla's mother, who slept with Clarence's father. The children didn't know that they were siblings until T J told the boy. It seems that he and the other uncle went over to confront him. He told them that he would kill Shayla and you too, Jacqueline. Well, the boy stole his uncle's car and went back. T J fired a shot at the boy and the boy killed him with his other uncle's gun."

"Oh my God," Yolanda said.

"Get this. The child, upset that the uncle hurt his beloved Mrs. Vance by killing her husband, had mixed emotions. He didn't like what Raphiel was doing to her either. Then no doubt when the uncle threatened to kill Jacqueline and Shayla, the boy did what he thought he needed to do."

"But if in fact, the uncle did shoot at the boy first, it could be self-defense."

"Yes, Lieutenant, you're right. I have the officers checking the car for the shot. But here's the problem, when he left the scene, he hit Sharon Smith, Shayla's mom. I guess she was on the way to try to find her daughter but Mr. Ratman from the shelter did say that she was high."

"That child's mother is on drugs," Jacqueline asked.

"Yes, and has been for some time. T J got her hooked for what she did to his sister. He took revenge into his own hands. He made Shayla turn tricks and cleans his drug houses to work off the drugs her mother used."

"Oh my goodness, that's why that child has been so bitter. That's why she's so mean. Lord, I didn't know." Jacqueline cried.

"Jacqueline, you were the only one who wouldn't give up on her. I'm the one ashamed." Yolanda said as she rubbed Jacqueline's hand.

"Furthermore, I've put Clarence into the juvenile center until I check out his story. If Sharon tests positive for drugs, there is a great possibility that she did walk out in front of the car. He was so scared that he didn't stop."

"This is so unfortunate. For his mother who's lost a brother. For Jacqueline who's lost a husband. And for that child who could very well lose her mother." Cheryl said.

"Well, I'm going to do everything in my power to see that Clarence is okay. I wished he would have come to the police but this happens with kids who have been around so much." Chief Jones said.

"I can't believe that Clarence would kill his own uncle to protect me. Can I go to see him, Chief Jones?"

"Yes, you can. I've also had someone to clean your home, Jacqueline. I don't know if you want to go there right now but you can if you'd like." Chief Jones said.

"No, I believe that I'll stay with mom and dad for a while. I am not ready to go back there. I do need to pick up some things. So daddy, if you don't mind, can you take me to the house and then over to see Clarence. In the morning I'm going to hire an attorney for him just in case."

"Okay baby, get your things while I walk Jones out," Hubert said to his daughter.

"Jones, do you think the boy is going to be okay?"

"Yes, Lieutenant, he seems to be a strong-minded young man. I would get him involved in some counseling if I were his mother."

"Well, she doesn't have too. I will. I will do whatever needs to be done for him. He loves Jacqueline and I am going to help him."

"I kind of figured you would." And both men started laughing.

JACQUELINE

Jacqueline went in to see Clarence Hines, who appeared to have been crying all night long. She felt so sorry for the young man who was a smart mouth.

Words couldn't describe the pain she felt for him.

"Clarence," she said and he lifted his head. Without saying a word he leaped up and put his arms around her neck.

"Mrs. Vance, I thought. I thought he had done something to you too."

"No, Clarence, I'm okay. Didn't I always tell you, children, that the Lord has my back."

"Yes, ma'am, but Mrs. Vance, he was going to hurt you too. You don't know my uncle. If he said he was going to do something, he did it."

"Yes, I believe you, Clarence, but I believe in God more. Do you remember when I told you that God has His angels encamped all around me?"

"I remember but because I couldn't see them, I guess I didn't believe it."

"Well, now, do you believe it?"

"Kind of, I know someone must be protecting you."

"God is. He is true to His word Clarence. Next time, I hope that you will come to me. If something ever happens, no matter what, come to me."

"Mrs. Vance, I didn't want to see you hurt. When my dad cheated on my mama, she was so sad. All she did was cry and there was nothing that I could say to help her. I didn't want you to feel that."

"I do thank you for being concerned for me. Remember this if you remember nothing else; there is no sorrow that heaven can't heal. No matter how hurt you may be, if you find solace in the word of God, you'll have peace. And, you will heal. I don't ever want you to jeopardize your own life trying to save mine."

"Mrs. Vance, you are the only teacher that put up with me and my jokes. You never curse me out or put me out of your class. No matter how terrible I am, you always try to encourage me. I remember everything you tell me. If I tell you something, will you promise not to tell anyone?"

"Yes, Clarence, I promise."

"When you give me those scriptures, I always wait until no one is around and I go to my mom's Bible and look them up. You are always right. What you said was right in the Bible."

"I have to study Clarence like I am always on you to study."

"I am going to study hard if I get out of this mess."

"Even if you didn't get out of this mess, you still ought to love Clarence. Love yourself enough to get every piece of information that your mind can contain. Wisdom is the best but knowledge is next in line."

"Yes, ma'am."

"Well, I have to go but I want you to know that I am praying for you. And like I promised to never tell your secret, you have to promise to go to church with me and your mom sometimes."

"I guess it wouldn't hurt."

"It won't hurt you at all. In fact, I can one hundred percent assure you it will help you."

"Okay, Mrs. Vance. As soon as I get out of here, I'm going to church."

"All right, baby, now give me a hug. And why don't we say a prayer before I leave."

"Okay but you have to pray," Clarence said, grabbing her outstretched hands.

"Father, we thank you for this day. Lord, we pray a special blessing on Clarence's life. Forgive him for his sins, save him, and Lord, whatever you do, keep Him. Lord, put some of your best angels around him while he's here and then please assign to him my angels when he leaves. We love you Lord and by faith, we believe in Jesus's name. Amen."

"Amen," Clarence said with a smile on his face.

After Jacqueline and Hubert left the juvenile center, Hubert drove them to her house. She waited until Hubert checked the surroundings before she got out of the car. He still couldn't be too careful about his little girl. To Hubert, it didn't matter how old Jacqueline was, she was still his little girl. When Jacqueline walked into the house she let out a sigh. It was too surreal.

Her husband was murdered at the home he built for her. She had no intentions of ever living there again. The sooner she could clear out her belongings, the sooner she would have peace. She took some things from her drawers. As she placed them on her bed she noticed a letter laying on the pillow. Jacqueline was halfway scared to pick it up.

Written across the front of the envelope said: Please Read This Jacqueline. Knowing that it was Raphiel's handwriting made her nervous. Nausea began to creep into her stomach. An overwhelming feeling of hysteria invaded her emotional state. As she held the letter in her hand, panic pushed its way in. A strong emotional collision tried to debauch all the Word she had hidden in her heart.

Jacqueline took a few deep breaths, collected her thoughts, and asked God to help her. Then she sat in the high back leopard chair next to her bed. She felt her hands tremble as she turned the envelope to open it. The envelope dangled in her shaking hands and Hubert caught it before it hit the floor. When he saw her name, he also knew Raphiel wrote it.

"Baby girl, would you like for me to read the letter to you?" he asked. Instead, you shook her head no and replied, "Daddy, it's something that I have to do by myself."

Although he didn't agree, he knew there wasn't any need for him to display a rebuttal from everything he'd taught her. He handed her the envelope and held on until she had a firm grip. Without saying another word, he took a seat on the corner of her bed.

She didn't say anything but she felt stronger now that her dad was there. Jacqueline opened the envelope and in it, was a letter…

Jacqueline, I apologize for the way that I've treated you. I haven't been honest to you or myself.

Sweetheart, I know that you were the best thing that ever happened to me. I couldn't see the beauty of your ocean for the trees that I'd grown over the years. Not only was my vision of your loveliness blocked, but also my ability to do what was right. I betrayed you and our marriage by sleeping with someone else.

I'm ashamed to even tell you who it was and that doesn't matter. All that matters now is that you know how sorrowful I am. I never thought that losing you would be so unbearable. But when you put me out last evening, I realized that without you, I am nothing. I became so engulfed in myself and the money that I made (which was our money) until I failed to see the joy that Jesus had already given me. It wasn't in the money, or the business, it was in the relationship that I'd built with you. I know that now that things are so torn apart that it was me; my entire fault.

I should have been blessed to have a wife who loved the Lord and always prayed for me. It was your prayers that covered me. Instead, I took your love and you for granted. Jacqueline, I've asked the Lord to forgive me of my sins and now I'm asking you to do the same. Whether we are together or apart, I'll always remember the way things used to be. The way you use to hold me and care for me. The way you loved me, even when I didn't love myself. I know that God is a forgiving God, but forever will I carry the burden of letting you down in my heart. Sweet Jacqueline,

I'm letting you go. Not because I don't love you anymore, but because I'm not worthy of your love. Asking you to wait for me feels crazy, but I don't want to lose you. I also don't know how long it's going to take for God to clean me up. Yet, I've decided to go away so that it won't be hard on you. I've put Vance's dealership in your name and all the money we had is still in the account.

I've taken a couple of the CDs we had so that I can have a little cash for my journey. Where I'm going, I don't have a clue. All I know is that I can't stand the thought of not coming home to you forever. Pray for me and remember if you wait, I'll be the happiest man on Earth, but if you decide to move on, I'll understand.

Know that for the rest of my life, you'll always be my wife. I love you. Forever and Always

Raphiel Vance

Jacqueline balled up into a knot in her bed and began to cry; it was the position she was growing accustomed to. Hubert decided that she needed this moment to grieve the husband that she'd loved. He vanished from the bedroom.

She cried because she loved him. Cried because she'd put him out. Most of all, she cried because she will never get a chance to tell him that she forgave him.

"God, if there is any way that You can give a message to Raphiel, please tell him that I will always love him and I forgive him."

Then she grabbed his pillow that still held the scent of his cologne and held it close to her. Right now she wanted to remember because tomorrow, she'd be letting him go. For some reason the letter made everything feel so different. She was happy that all her thoughts of Raphiel in hell were now banished. Not only did Raphiel get a chance to ask God for forgiveness, he asked her as well.

BRADLEY

Bradley sat in his recliner with the lights dimmed. He put on some soft tunes that were flowing in the atmosphere from his surround sound system. Nights like tonight he longed to have someone he could call a companion. It wasn't often that he felt this way but lately, thoughts of Jacqueline were bombarding his mind.

He decided that a nice shower would channel his thoughts back to reality. He grabbed his pajamas and hurried to the shower. As he was about to run the water he heard the sound of the telephone.

"Hello, Mrs. Burch." He knew it was her because he looked at his caller identification hoping that it was Jacqueline.

"Hey, Bradley, did you watch the news tonight?"

"I didn't. I've had all the drama that I can stand for one week."

"They solved Vance's murder. The young man who killed Raphiel Vance died today on Pete Street. One of the ladies from the church said that his very own nephew killed him. The boy was trying to keep his teacher, Jacqueline Vance safe."

Bradley shook his head. "You've got to be kidding me. Even young men realize how special that lady is."

Mrs. Burch giggled. "I guess so. You know her dad was a lieutenant in the police department. I heard he did whatever he could to help the young boy out and they determined the killing as self defense."

"All I know is that I'm glad that child is okay."

"Me too. Well, where is my baby?"

"She's sleeping like an angel."

"Okay, I thought I'd let you know. They said that the graveside service for her husband will be tomorrow at noon."

"Thanks, Mrs. Burch. Have a good night now."

"You too, son."

Bradley realized that in her own little slick way, Mrs. Burch was doing herself some matchmaking. He wondered if it would be appropriate for him to attend being that he didn't know the fellow. Then he decided that he did know Jacqueline and if for nothing else than to show her that he cared, he was going.

He prolonged his shower to shop in his closet for the perfect suit and tie. He pulled out his latest masterpiece by Sean John and found a matching tie to go with his selection. If Denise had taught him nothing else, she taught him how to look good and definitely how to smell good.

YOLANDA

Yolanda decided that since the disaster was over, she needed to go home. She hadn't been feeling well at all and had attributed stress for the cause. One of the officers stationed at the ranch received orders to take her home. He was also told to remain at her apartment on watch which was a relief to her.

The thought of that Hines boy stealing the keys from his sister's job spooked her. He could have been in her apartment and she didn't even know it. For Yolanda, this certified her feeling that it was moving time.

Although she wanted to be at Big L's, *well Raphiel's*, graveside service she decided it wouldn't be good for Jacqueline. As the officer drove her home, he made candid small talk with her. She appreciated his efforts to lift her spirits but she figured she had the right to be sad.

After all, the man she'd fallen in love with was using her to hurt his wife. She never had the chance to tell him how she felt. That would have made him come to terms with the pain he'd be causing her.

Officer James walked around the house to make sure everything was secure. She offered to make him a cup of coffee but he'd refused her offer. He asked her if she was hungry and she remembered that she hadn't eaten all day. Her stomach had been far too queasy to eat earlier but now she was starving.

His daughter worked at the pizza parlor not far from her apartment, so he called to order a pizza. He didn't take her up on her offer to stay inside but instead went and sat in his patrol car.

As she walked from room to room, she couldn't help but remember the man she'd fallen for. She was in dire need of relaxation. She went into her bathroom to run a hot bubble bath. As she was about to close the bathroom door, she noticed a letter in the center of her bed.

Her heart skipped a beat when she saw her name written on the envelope. She didn't have a clue whom the letter was from but the flitters in her stomach were evidence of her nervousness. She opened the envelope and in it was two letters and a check. She sat down so she could read...

Dear Yolanda,

I must be truthful with you. I am a married man who's been going through so much. Not that my wife put me through, but I put myself through. I didn't realize the beauty of having a woman who loved the Lord until she put me out.

At first, it didn't matter because I felt like I had you to fall on. Then I realized that I'd betrayed not only my wife, but you as well. You have known my wife for some time. I sought you because I knew that if you and I ever had an affair, it would tear her apart. Unfortunately, I'm the one who's torn apart.

As I looked at the deceit that I engaged in, I remembered when Judas betrayed Jesus. He could find no comfort with living and I don't want to be like him. I've asked the Lord to forgive me, my wife, and now I'm asking you to forgive me.

You are a wonderful woman and it's not that you don't want to love; you have a hard time trying to pick who to love. Yolanda, let love find you. You have so much to offer and the man who finds you will find a good thing, and something worth holding on too.

I pray that you'll find a place in your heart to forgive me. I'm going away to clear my head and establish a relationship with God.

It is my plan to come back to my wife if she'll have me. I know that I've cost you some pain and maybe even a lasting friendship. Enclosed you'll find a check for four hundred and fifty thousand dollars.

It's part of a trust fund that I've never used. I'm giving you this money. I have a feeling that our relationship will be much more complicated than you think.

I'm not going to tell you what I mean because no matter what, I want you to decide and I'll accept that. Again, I apologize for the pain I've caused you. I came to you looking for the shallow being I thought you were but I found someone who was not at all shallow. I found someone who was full of adventure, full of love, and full of life.

Take Care of Yourself,
Raphiel Vance

Officer Johnny James sat in his patrol car. There had been something interesting about that woman from the moment he'd laid eyes on her. She was tall, beautiful, and feisty; everything he wanted in a woman. He thought that he'd better sit in his car because he couldn't be responsible for anything he'd do to her.

For ten years he had been praying for God to send him a wife. He knew that he'd know her the moment he saw her, and he did. Yolanda is the woman he wanted to spend the rest of his life with. He'd known in extensive details how Raphiel had betrayed her. He didn't want to be a rebound guy because what he had in store for her was a lifestyle and a life change.

He wanted to take her away from this apartment and put her in his five-bedroom home. It echoed because of loneliness and he wanted a family.

"God if she is the one, please show me some kind of sign," he murmured. His daughter tapping on the window interrupted his thoughts.

"Hi, Dad, you must have a date or something."

"No, I don't have a date but the woman who I am protecting was hungry."

"Yeah right, I see something in your eyes that you intend on doing more than feeding her."

"Girl, goodbye."

"Bye, Dad, I love you."

"I love you too, and don't forget to…"

"Lock those doors," she finished his sentence and they laughed. She knew what he was going to say, and he knew she was always prepared to hear it. He watched his daughter drive away and then he took a deep breath. When he made it to the top of the stairs, he heard crying. He eased the door open and sat the pizza on the table. He pulled his gun out of the holster because if someone was hurting Yolanda, he'd been more than prepared to use it.

Yolanda didn't know what to think. Here she was trying to hate the man who'd almost cost her a wonderful friendship. Now, she found herself in a place of forgiveness that she'd never been in. Jacqueline had forgiven her and she had to forgive him. Tears began to overtake her.

She wept for the love she'd felt, for his betrayal, and for the change that was going on inside of her. Officer James eased her bedroom door open only to find her alone and crying. He immediately secured his gun back in its place and rushed in beside her.

"Come on now. Whatever it is, God can solve it. You let it all out so when it's over you'll be able to smile."

She was so happy that he was there. She laid her head in the lock of his arm and cried until she couldn't cry anymore. His propitious manner gave her the force she needed to keep her from wallowing in pity.

He'd been a phenomenal gentleman and she was much obliged. He took a handkerchief from her nightstand and dried her eyes. The look of deep concern in his eyes pricked her heart.

"Are you okay now?"

"I thank God that you were here. Read this." And James read the letter. It sort of upset him but this man was dead but at least he'd done the honorable thing and apologized.

"Yolanda, I'm sorry that you had to go through this situation. But he did get some things right. You are a beautiful woman and you are going to be a wonderful wife. You've never had a man to tell you how beautiful you are."

"Thank you, Officer James."

"Would you please call me Johnny?"

"Yes, Johnny," she said without reaction.

"Well, I know you're hungry. How about some pizza?"

"I am hungry right now so that will be great."

"You sit right here and I'll bring you something to eat. By the way, do you have anything to drink?"

"There might be some drinks in the refrigerator. Why don't you look in there and see?"

"I sure will."

Yolanda had never been in the company of a man so caring. Neither had she been with one who wasn't trying to get laid, or had genuine concern. She smiled at the thought of a man in her kitchen looking for something to drink.

Generally the only thing she bought to drink was alcohol, but lately, she hadn't been able to drink that. The last time she'd been out, she bought herself a drink. Before it hit her throat, she was in the ladies room throwing up. That had never happened before. She decided that her stomach was telling her that she'd been drinking too much.

Johnny came around the corner smiling with two glasses of ice water in his hands. Yolanda laughed because she was even surprised that he found that.

"I see now that I am going to have to teach you how to shop."

"Somebody needs too." And they both laughed.

"Well, on a serious note, has this guy messed things up for the next guy?"

"I kind of decided to finally allow the Lord to have me to be found. I kind of made up my mind to leave my past far behind me."

"I see. Was it that bad?"

"I would call it careless. I decided that I had to have a certain type of guy. I especially didn't want anyone with children and the baby mama drama. So I guess I became picky and selfish."

"You're not the only one who's been that way. I promise you after my first marriage, I thought I knew the signs to keep me from going through the same things. Unfortunately, I turned a lot of good women down and I've been alone for ten years now. You don't know how tired I am of going to the big house I built for a family, alone."

"Trust me, this apartment might not be as big as your house but I promise you it's as lonely."

"So what are your plans now?" Johnny asked, hoping that she would say, "To move in with you."

"I know that tomorrow, I'm calling the movers. Where I'm going, I haven't quite decided yet. Jacqueline told me I could come to stay with her but I don't want to impose."

"Here's an idea, I know you don't know me but you can ask Lieutenant Collins about me. He's a good judge of character and if you know him, you know the man never lies."

"He does tell the truth even if it hurts," Yolanda said.

"Yes, but he wants the best for people. Well, as I was saying, why don't you move in with me? No strings attached. I'm always working but I can promise that you'll be safe. It'll be good to have some company around."

"Can you let me pray about it?"

"Not only will I let you pray, but I'll also pray with you."

"Right now."

"I don't know a better time than the present."

"Okay. I'll start off and I guess you can finish."

"Sounds like a plan to me." And they both kneeled down beside her bed. As she was about to start, he reached over and grabbed her hand.

"Lord, I know you have heard from me more in these last few days than You ever have, but now I know that I need you. I need direction and I know you know. Please direct my path. Show me the next steps in my life that You'd have me to take. Your word says that the steps of a good man are ordered by You. Would you order my steps?" And she paused, and then Johnny started.

"Father, we are touching and agreeing in Your name and we know you are in the midst. Nothing just happens and that I am my sisters' keeper. Would you touch Yolanda's heart so that she'll accept the things that You have in store for her? Mend her heart where it's broken, and reconstruct her mind where doubt may be. You will because whatever we ask in Your name will be given unto us. Bind us closer as we rejoice in the friendship You've created between us. We thank you and we love you, Lord, in Jesus's name. Amen."

Yolanda was sure of one thing when she got up off her knees, that God had sent a true man into her life. Her grandfather used to say, "A good man doesn't mind going on bended knees with his woman." She knew by this that Johnny was a good man. Then she decided to ask him a question. Whether his answer is correct would determine where her boxes would get shipped.

"Johnny, do you go to church?"

"I wouldn't miss it even if I wanted to," he answered, blushing because he saw the smile on her face.

SHAYLA

Shayla stood horrified looking at her mother who appeared lifeless. As tears began to roll down her face she grabbed Sharon by the hand.

"Mama, if you can hear me it's Shayla. I love you, Mama. Please don't leave me," she begged, feeling an emptiness that she'd never felt before.

"Come on, baby girl, you got to be strong. I bet she hears you and she's saying stop crying," Mr. Ratman said. As Shayla buried her face in his chest, he motioned for her to look. Sharon had opened her eyes. One tear slid down the side of her face connecting with her ear. Shayla wiped the tears and kissed her mother's cheek. Then Sharon tried to speak.

"Mama will be fine. The Lord...has given me... another...chance to get...things right. I'm so...sorry for all...the pain I've caused...you," Sharon struggled to say.

"It's all right, Mama. I love you. I know you were sick." Shayla tried to get her mother to see that she was forgiven.

"I...want you to know...that I love you," she said before closing her eyes again.

"I love you too," Shayla said as she bent down to kiss her again.

"Come on, my girl, let's go home and we'll come back tomorrow."

"Okay but I want to be here early, Mr. Ratman," Shayla demanded.

"Early," he answered.

JACQUELINE

Jacqueline put on her black suit and found her matching hat and purse to match. She and Hubert had made it back to the ranch late last night. He allowed her all the time she needed to grieve for her husband. It seemed as if Jacqueline emerged from her bedroom a new woman.

She became determined to not let death steal the happy moments she'd spent with Raphiel. She also knew that Yolanda had a right to be there as she did. So she picked up the phone to call her.

"Hello there," Jacqueline said when Yolanda answered.

"Hello, Jacqueline, how are you?"

"I'm hanging in there. What about you?"

"My feelings don't matter."

"Yes, they do. If they didn't Raphiel wouldn't have tried to make things right. Did you read the letter he left you?"

"How did you know?"

"He forwarded a copy of your letter in my envelope."

"Are you okay with the money he left me? If not, I'll give it to you."

"Don't you dare! For the pain he caused you, that's the least we can do. I'd never even dream of taking it from you. It's yours. Don't think he didn't leave me any. He made sure I never had to work ever again."

"Looks like he still turned out to be a class act." And the women laughed.

"I guess you could call it that. Hey, you need to be dressing for the service."

"Jacqueline, I wouldn't impose on you like that. You've already done more than enough."

"Don't do it for me, Yolanda, do it for you. You know if you don't go, there will always be a part of you that wished you would have gone. I'm going there to say goodbye to his remains and start my life all over again."

"You don't have to start again, pick up right where God has you, Jacqueline."

"Thanks but you need to say goodbye too. I hope you make the right decision and come. By the way, Johnny called me and dad last night. He's a good man Yolanda and you'd be a fool to let him slip away."

"I kind of feel like he's special. I was thinking things might be moving too fast."

"Girl, anytime God is in something, it doesn't take long. Let go and let God. I love you and I'll see you at the graveyard."

"Okay," Yolanda said and hung up the phone.

Yolanda found herself a nice black dress and put it on. She found some cute jewelry to enhance the dress that was plain and simple. It was her intention to reflect any light that might be pointing in her direction. When she picked up her keys, someone knocked at the door. She wasn't expecting any visitors so the knock kind of startled her.

"Who is it?" she asked.

"Someone who doesn't want you to do anything alone." the voice answered, and she immediately knew who it was.

"Hey, pretty lady. I thought I'd go with you to the graveside service. Now folks won't be speculating because your man will be on your side."

"Thank you, Johnny, for being so thoughtful," she said as she wrapped her arms in his extended arm.

"The movers will be here to gather your things at twelve. I've already told them where to put everything and we'll sort things out whenever you like."

"Thank you. I've never had anyone so thoughtful in my life."

"You do now, sweet lady," he said before kissing her hand and placing her in his washed vehicle.

⸙

"Cheryl, Jacqueline, it's time to go," Hubert yelled from the front door.

"Okay, Daddy. I'm coming," Jacqueline yelled back.

"Be there in a moment," Cheryl added.

Then Hubert shook his head as his two beautiful women came front and center at the same exact time. He remembered the past when he had both of them home together. Some way or another, they always managed to make him late for everything. He smiled at the thought and moved to the side so that the ladies could pass by him. Then after he locked the house, he ran to the car before them and opened both the front and back passenger doors.

He'd been taught that a man should always open doors for women. As he instructed his two women to put their seatbelts on, he got into the driver seat. They proceeded on the journey set before them.

BRADLEY

Bradley got up and dressed Denisia. He had never taken her to a funeral before. Jacqueline loved Denisia and seeing her may give her a much needed dose of happiness. This also would be a great opportunity for him to finally take her to Denise's grave. Gripping agony over his loss had caused him to neglect to take her. Today, he wouldn't have dared gone that close and not taken any flowers.

By the time they made it to the graveside service, Jacqueline was singing. It was as though an angel was serenading the people of God. After she finished, she thanked the tearful crowd for showing so much support, and then she took her seat.

Before Bradley could catch her, Denisia broke away from his grip and ran to Jacqueline. Despite her tears she looked down and immediately picked the child up and put her in her lap. She held on to Denisia as if she was holding on to her very own child.

When the service concluded, Jacqueline still had Denisia, as the people came to greet her. She stood with one hand extended for handshakes and hugs, as the other held firm to the small child's hand. Then after everyone was gone through the line, Bradley stood in front of Jacqueline.

"Hi there, I'm so sorry for your loss and I especially apologize for this little girl."

"Oh please, no apology needed. I was so happy to see her!" she said pinching Denisia's nose and smiling at Bradley.

"Come on, meet my parents. Mom and Dad, this is the special family that I told you about. The ones I met at the theater."

"Hi, son," Hubert Collins said in his protective daddy's voice. Then he reached down and took Denisia in his arms. It wasn't long before he had her introducing herself to all the police officers coming to shake his hand.

"Hi, Bradley," Cheryl said. Jacqueline and Bradley looked at her. Jacqueline, surprised she'd remembered his name. And Bradley, surprised that Jacqueline had even told her.

"It's a pleasure to meet you and Deni..." Cheryl said and Bradley helped her with the ending.

"S-ia. Thank you and the pleasure is all mine," Bradley replied.

Jacqueline placed her hand on his shoulder. "I'm so happy that you all came today. I needed her."

Bradley looked into her eyes. "I thought that you might be in need of a friend or two."

"I need all the support that I can get. Are you coming out to the ranch for dinner?"

"Only if we're invited," he said, hoping that it was an invitation.

Jacqueline blushed. "You are and I would love to have you two as my special guests."

"We're there, but you have to give me directions."

She giggled. "I can do one better. If you don't mind, I can catch a ride with you and Denisia and I'll point you in the direction."

"That's fine with me but I was going to take Denisia to her mother's grave since we were so close. I thought I would take some flowers. I would be happy to have a friend with me," Bradley confessed, hoping that she would go with them.

"Are you sure?" Jacqueline asked, this time looking him in his eyes as though to make sure he meant what he said.

Bradley never wavered. "Yes, I'm positive."

"After everyone leaves, we can go," Jacqueline said.

Bradley pointed toward his car. "I'll wait by the car." Bradley felt happy and relieved that she'd decided to go along. The little hand tapping on his leg meant Denisia had questions of her own.

"Can I stay with Jacqueline, Daddy?" Denisia asked.

"What did you say, young lady?" Bradley asked with that stern daddy look.

"I apologize," she corrected herself and then finished, "but can I stay with Ms. Jacqueline, Daddy?"

"PawPaw said I can come to his ranch and ride his horse."

Bradley and Jacqueline both started laughing.

"I apologize, Bradley. He's as anxious to be a PawPaw as she is to ride the horse." They both laughed and he turned his attention back to his daughter.

"Only if Mrs. Jacqueline doesn't mind," he replied.

"I don't mind at all. And she had it right, it's Ms. Jacqueline." Jacqueline grabbed Denisia's hand in hers. They turned and walked over to say goodbye to the rest of her guests leaving Bradley alone to walk to his car.

"Jacqueline, you always find a child somewhere." Yolanda smiled down at Denisia.

"Denisia, this is Ms. Clark."

The child extended her hand toward Yolanda. "Hello, Ms. Clark. My name is Denisia Johnson."

Yolanda accepted the little hand and gave it a gentle shake. "Well, it's a pleasure to meet you, Ms. Denisia. I wish you could come teach my class how to be polite."

"The pleasure is all mine. And I will teach them everything I know." Denisia said and the two women snickered.

"Thank you for coming, Yolanda. I know this was hard for you, but I know that this bridge you had to cross. With the help of the Lord, together we can now face new ones."

Yolanda threw her arms around her friend. "Thank you, Jacqueline. I needed to be here like you said. Now, I can move on as God would want me to."

Jacqueline looked at her friend with pure amazement. *This chick said as God would want her to. Won't the Lord do it?* She giggled. "I see He's already put a knight in shining armor in your path."

Yolanda grabbed her free hand as she used the other to hold the little hand next to her. "Girl, I have never had a man to treat me the way Johnny is treating me. He's been my second rock next to the Lord who is my first rock."

"You don't know how happy I am to hear you say that. Everything is going to be fine and I mean everything. Are you and Johnny going to the ranch?"

"Yes, Mr. Collins already asked him and he said yes. You know I'm moving my things over to his house. He offered to let me stay until I found a place of my own."

Jacqueline puckered her lips. "Girl, please. Johnny James isn't going to let you leave his house. And it is beautiful too. You better think about a color scheme because he chose to leave the walls white until he got married."

A tear ran down Yolanda's face. "Do you think it's my time?"

"Yes, I do believe that it's your time." Jacqueline swiped her friend's tears away, released Denisia's hand, and hugged Yolanda tight.

"Well, looks like you have yourself a potential situation brewing too. Jacqueline, enjoy him and her," Yolanda looked down at Denisia and pinched her cheek. "You've been a perfect wife and now it's time for you to move on as well."

Jacqueline smiled and whispered, "I'm not quite ready to date yet. But I am looking forward to everything God has planned for me."

"I love you, Jacqueline and whatever you decide, I'll always be here for you."

"I love you too, Yolanda, and you can count on me forever too."

"See you at the ranch."

"Okay."

Bradley stood far off watching Jacqueline, his daughter, and Yolanda.

"Lord, if this is the woman for me, please let me find favor with her."

She was so graceful and full of life.

Even at a time in her life when she could very well break down, she didn't. It was evident that she was in the arms of the Master. Everywhere she went, she held on to Denisia's hand and she did likewise.

It was so wonderful to see his daughter with someone who had the instincts of such a nurturing mother. When the last car was driving away and the two walked toward his car, his heart skipped a beat. He knew right then and there that God was answering his prayers

JACQUELINE

All the family and friends of Raphiel and Jacqueline gathered at the Collins' family ranch for the repast. Everyone talked and mingled amongst themselves. Some were wondering where Jacqueline had disappeared to. No one was crazy enough to ask questions because Hubert was known for making you never want to be noisy again. He believed that not only did people need to run their own business, but others needed to shut their mouths.

"Jacqueline, this is my wife's grave site," Bradley said as they laid the flowers in the vase on Denise's tombstone.

"Daddy, is there where my mommy is?"

"What did I tell you about Mommy?"

"You said that Mommy was sleeping in the arms of Jesus and that her body was here but her spirit was with the Lord."

"That's right," he said as he grabbed his daughter and brought her closer in his arms. "Okay, we better go now."

"Are you sure, Bradley? You've only been here a little while." Jacqueline asked.

"Jacqueline, I'm convinced that Denise was never here. I put her remains here but she has been and is with the Lord. I only wanted to bring flowers since I was so close. I never want my child to visit here or feel obligated to come here. This is no place for people who have peace about death. She loved Christ, she believed, and I know that she will live again."

"I understand. I'm ready when you are."

"Daddy look, there's a white bird sitting on Mommy's grave." Denisia said, pointing at the most beautiful white dove either of them had ever seen.

"He knows that's where the remains of an angel lay," Bradley said, holding Denisia in his arms. He reached over and took Jacqueline by the hand. He opened the car door for Jacqueline and then buckled Denisia in the back seat. When he came around to his side, he was thankful Jacqueline had taken the liberty to reach over and open his door. As she put her seatbelt on, he noticed that she had the prettiest hands.

He started the car and they were on their way. The grave site was only fifteen minutes away from the ranch. When they arrived, most of the guests were already sitting down with their plates. The food smelled delicious and the way people were eating, Bradley figured that it would taste just as good. Hubert Collins greeted them and took Denisia to the den to play with the other children. Then he guided Bradley to a seat in the living room and sat down beside him.

Hubert looked at Bradley, "Where's your daughter's mother, son?"

"My wife died three years ago from a car accident. She was pregnant with Denisia at the time and I lost a wife but gained a daughter."

Hubert put his hand on her shoulder. "I'm sorry to hear that. I heard about your story though. I was still a lieutenant with the police department then."

Bradley nodded. "Okay. And now?"

"Now I'm a retired policeman but a bonafide rancher," Hubert said with dignity.

"Well, I own Tequila Delights, the liquor store down on Jewella Avenue."

"Yes, I know the place well."

"It was my dream to own something and I chose it since I bought it at a steal. Unfortunately, lately, I've been thinking that it is the wrong business for me."

"What brought that on, son?"

"See, I got saved three years ago when Denise got killed. Before, I was like all the other thirty something year olds you might know. Now, I don't feel right serving alcohol." Bradley said before their conversation got interrupted by a familiar face.

"Hey, Bradley, how are you?"

"Hey, Yolanda, everything is fine. I haven't seen you in the store lately."

"No, things are changing and I doubt if you will see me anytime soon. There's something going on with my stomach and alcohol. I can't even stand the way it smells."

"I'm sorry I'm losing a good customer, but I'm happy for you. I didn't believe that a lady as pretty as you should be drinking as much as you did."

"Thanks. I don't know whether to feel bad or good."

"Oh, don't take it as something bad. I'm glad that you've made a good decision that seems to fit you better."

"That's not the only good decision that I've made. I've rededicated my life back to Christ." This time Bradley stood to his feet to embrace Yolanda.

"I'm so proud of you. Now, you are my sister in Christ!" Bradley shouted. Everyone in the room sort of looked in their direction to see what all the commotion was about. When Bradley realized that everyone was looking his way he said, "Hey, this sister came back to the Lord!" And everyone started to applaud and hug her in splendid congratulations.

Hubert had never seen anyone operate a room this smooth except for Pastor Hunt. This young man had an anointing on his life and it showed. There was no doubt that he'd turned what could very well have been a time of mourning into a complete celebration. Hubert knew that one thing would set this house on fire. His baby girl's voice. He motioned for Jacqueline to come to him and began singing a song she wrote.

"†When one comes to Christ the angels rejoice,
†When one comes to Christ it's the most perfect choice,

†I'm so glad you came, so glad, So glad that you came.
†Hallelujah! You've found your way back home,
†Hallelujah! Doesn't matter that you've been gone,
†I'm so glad you came, so glad, so glad that you came."

When Jacqueline finished everyone was crying and praising God. Bradley had heard a little of her singing voice at the grave but she was at the end of the song.

Now he heard the fullness of her gift and it was a gift. There almost wasn't a dry eye in the room. Everyone else was as mesmerized as he was. Hubert nonetheless, was a proud papa. You could see the distinct look of admiration in his eyes toward his one and only daughter.

Jacqueline was glad that the mood had been set on worship. Everyone was worshiping God and the love that flowed through the house was pure and evident.

She was so happy that Yolanda finally had a man who was trying to get with her. And not because of a sexual experience but because of her beauty both on the inside and outside. She was also grateful that the worshiping gave Geraldine some much needed relief. She'd cried the whole service because of sadness and now she was rejoicing.

SHAYLA'S MOM

Sharon was an ineradicable lady. She'd made an overnight turn-around. The doctors made the decision to take her out of the intensive care unit and put her in her very own room. Her progress was miraculous.

There was no denying she was already blessed beyond measure. She'd sustained only one broken rib, a slight concussion, and a broken arm. Others have died from the kind of hit she took and there was no mistake whether God spared her life.

She awaited her daughter's visit so that she could see that she was no longer in the intensive care unit. Sharon was still sort of sketchy on the details of how she'd gotten there in the first place. Although she had plenty of questions to ask, if she didn't find out anything, it didn't matter.

There was one thing that she was sure of; she was thankful. Thankful to be alive and thankful she had a second chance at life.

Sharon sat up in her bed when she heard the nurse pointing someone to her room. She hoped it was Shayla. When the door opened the shock of who it was evident on her face. It was her old friend who she'd betrayed.

"Hello, Sharon. I'm so grateful that you're alive."

"Hi, Hattie, I'm grateful too. I know that Clarence wasn't trying to hit me. I've already told the cops that I was high and didn't realize that I'd walked into the streets."

"I know and that's why I'm here. Because of your testimony my son is now free. I want to tell you thanks."

"There's no need."

"Yes, there is. I am at fault for why you were high in the first place. I hated you for sleeping with my husband and when I found out that you were pregnant, it liked to have killed me. I didn't realize that I was transferring all my emotions in the atmosphere. And my brother, he was soaking up the anger like a sponge. I didn't believe that he would set out to hurt you and Shayla like this."

"Hattie, that's not your fault. Everyone makes their own choices, even me. There have been so many times that I could have turned away from drugs, but I didn't. I don't know if it was not having enough power, or not wanting to break the habit. And although T J played a part in it, it was still up to me. I didn't feel like I had anything to keep me from drugs when all I needed was the will to live and my baby."

"I'm happy that now you can make some changes," Hattie said.

"I sure can but not of my own will. I used to try to change myself Hattie and every time, I failed. I know now that God is the one who changes people and I've finally asked Him to change me. I have power because now I'm in the will of God."

"Sounds good to me. I'm proud of you. Sharon, I want you to know you hurt me back then, but that's all over now. I want Clarence and Corey to know their sister. Shayla needs to know that she has brothers that she can depend on."

"I'm so glad that you feel that way. I was waiting for her to tell her everything. I didn't want my baby to ever think that she was a mistake. I love her, Hattie, and she's all I have. I was so wrong for sleeping with your husband, but God knew. He knew that this moment would come and I'd fight hard because Shayla was more than enough to live for. Well Shayla and my desire to tell you I'm so sorry for what I did to you."

"I forgive you, Sharon. I forgave you a long time ago. I had to in order for me to do the things God wanted me to do. I almost let unforgiveness block my blessings. I now realize that if God forgives me daily, I can forgive you. Well, I needed to say these things. I better get going."

"Thank you for coming, Hattie. Everything will be alright and hey, may God bless you."

"You too, Sharon; goodbye." And Hattie left the hospital room.

JACQUELINE

After everyone had left, except for Bradley and Denisia, Cheryl made a fresh pot of coffee. All four adults sat at the table. Denisia was in the living room watching cartoons on the big flat screen television. Hubert and Bradley talked about everything from fishing to business. Cheryl was very impressed with Bradley and expressed her feelings to Jacqueline. She already knew he was a special man. She'd known from the day they met. She still had no intentions on getting involved with anyone.

Jacqueline decided to take a break from her mother's pushing to go in to check on Denisia. The little beauty was asleep on the sofa. She wondered if Bradley would consider staying at the ranch. since there was plenty of room for the both of them. She took Denisia up to her room and put her on one of her very own childhood nightgowns that was in a chest at the foot of her bed.

Cheryl had been so sentimental about her things until she'd kept a nightgown or two from every age. Then she tucked Denisia in her bed and kissed her on the forehead. She went downstairs to let Bradley know where his little girl was. He was still rambling on and on with Hubert. Neither of them seemed to have noticed she and Cheryl had left them there.

"Excuse me, gentlemen. Denisia is upstairs in my bed, Bradley. I wondered, since we have so much room, would the two of you like to stay here tonight?"

"Oh yeah, that would be good," Hubert said, shaking his head. He was so happy to have some male company that he considered good company.

"I guess that would be okay. It's not like we have anyone waiting on us at home." Bradley said and Jacqueline laughed at him.

Neither one of us had anyone waiting at home, right now. But somehow deep within Jacqueline knew things would change.

YOLANDA

Yolanda and Johnny made it to his home. Yolanda was so happy that the day was over and that it had gone as well as it has. She still felt so sorry for Raphiel's aunt who cried most of the day. Anyone could see that he meant so much more to her than a nephew.

Yolanda pulled off her shoes before she got into the house. Her feet were kind of swollen from being on them most of the day. She'd help Mrs. Collins serve the entire guest visitors and there were lots of them.

"Is everything okay?" Johnny asked as he watched Yolanda's face grow from tired to mournful.

"I was thinking about Raphiel's aunt. She was so hurt and I pray that all is well with her."

"Well, little lady, why don't we do something about it? Come on, let's pray for her."

"Okay." She said looking strange at the man. He had to believe in prayer because he would pray at the drop of a situation. Anytime something or someone required prayer, he was willing, ready, and able.

"Father, we bow before you to say, "Thank You." We thank you for this day and all that you have done. You said that man ought to always pray and that we should pray for one another. So Yolanda and I bow asking you to touch Ms. Geraldine. Mend her heart Lord because we know that it's broken. Show her that hope will prevail and that you are her blessed hope. We thank you in Jesus's name. Amen."

As they both got up from their knees. They were facing each other. Johnny took the liberty to plant a long gentle kiss on Yolanda and she almost fainted. Not only did the man pray until heaven heard, he kissed like no one she'd ever kissed before.

"Thank you Johnny." She said not knowing what to say.

"For what? The prayer or the kiss?" He asked.

"Actually, for everything Mr. Funny. No one has ever been this kind to me and I wanted to tell you I appreciate everything."

"I know you do. Yolanda, I can see how happy you are in your eyes. I have a surprise so I guess there's no better time than now to give it to you. I know that you also took this coming week off of work and so did I. I've planned a three day get-away so you can relax. Clear your mind of everything here. How does that sound?"

Yolanda leaped into his arms like a two year old. She so wanted and needed to get gone. She had no idea where she would go but now that he's done all the deciding for her, there was no limit to the gratitude she felt.

Johnny held her. He was so blessed to have her in his home, and now in his life. He didn't know that his surprise was going to get this much of a response but he was happy it had. In his first marriage, he never did these types of things.

He made a vow that if God ever put another woman in his life; he would give her as much of the world as he could. They only had three days but he intended to make the best of them. He'd already purchased their tickets and they were scheduled to leave for Ft. Lauderdale right after Sunday service.

SHAYLA

Shayla opened the door to her mother's hospital room. Sharon was asleep so Shayla pulled a chair close to her bed and sat there. Mr. Ratman had decided to go to the cafeteria to get them some snacks before coming up.

They both were so excited when they found out that Sharon was no longer in intensive care. The doctors told them that she is a walking miracle. Now as Shayla sat watching her mother, she thought about how pretty she was.

It had been so hard to see her beauty in the past. The fact that she was high always overshadowed the good things about her. As Shayla motioned to get up, Sharon opened her eyes.

"Hey there, girl, I called myself waiting for you to get here, but I fell asleep."

"Hey, Mama, you did. You were even snoring when I came in here."

"Girl, stop that. You know I don't snore."

Shayla bent over and kissed her mom before replying, "Oh yes, you do." And they laughed.

"Where's Mr. Ratman?"

Shayla giggled. "He went downstairs to grab us some snacks. Mama, he likes you. He's been the greatest. It's almost like I have a daddy."

Shayla sat down in the chair beside her mother's bed. *It feels good to have a daddy.*

Sharon smiled, "I'm happy that you like him that much."

"I do and he's even helped me with all my homework. When I go back to school Monday, I'll have all my stuff done."

"That's good Shayla. Look, Mommy has something to tell you. First, I want you to know that there will be no more drugs in my life. The spirit of addition has ruled and stolen from me, too long. With the help of the Lord, some church, and some meetings, I'm going to beat this. Second, I want to tell you again that I am sorry for putting you through this mess. There was so much pressure on you to be a mother to your mother, and that wasn't right. I should have been the one taking care of you. Last but not least, you have two brothers. Their names are Clarence and Corey Hines. Their father was your father."

Shayla stared at her mother. She knew she'd heard her, but she had to repeat what she said to make her brain understand. "Mom, Clarence and Corey Hines are my brothers?"

"Yes, sweetheart, and their mother came to see me today."

"Really? What did she want?" Shayla looked at her mother as if she could read her brain. She'd had all the drama she could stand and if this woman came with drama, she was going to cut this demon's head off.

"Calm down, Scrappy Doo," Sharon knew Shayla's facial expression well. And this particular face was the feisty one that will fight anybody. "She wants you guys to be brother and sister. We've kept you all apart for too long because of how we felt but now, you have family. Shayla, I know you don't know this but family is everything."

"Mom, you know Clarence and I have classes together. He always gave me money and he always took care of me for some reason."

"Yeah, Clarence may have known but you didn't know."

"Ah, man! I have two brothers!" Shayla shouted.

"You do," Sharon smiled.

"Hey in here, I can hear you all the way down the hall girl."

"Mr. Ratman, guess what?"

"What, girl?"

"I have two brothers; Clarence and Corey."

"That's awesome."

"And guess what else I have?"

"What might that be, you happy teenager?"

"I have a new and improved Mom and a dad."

Mr. Ratman's heart sank when Shayla said that she had a Dad. Ratman's wife divorced him years ago when he opened the shelter. She'd said he spent too much time helping drunks and drug addicts for her. During the first couple of years, he'd begged her to have a child but she wouldn't hear of it.

She was too preoccupied with her fabulous lifestyle to have it interrupted with a child. After long nights and hard fights, she left. Ratman had never remarried and decided that the shelter was all he needed.

Until Sharon and Shayla walked in. He'd tried to get Sharon to come to meetings but she wouldn't. He'd realized that Shayla was more or less taking care of her mother. He decided that God put them in Ratman's House so he could help. He started off letting her help the kitchen cooks and then he taught her how to log the people in and out. Shayla had become the daughter he never had.

When he was getting used to the thought and had made provisions to move her and Sharon to his home, she found her dad.

"I'm happy for you young lady," he struggled to say. He was happy for her but he wasn't happy with the thought that she'd be leaving his life.

"Aren't you going to ask me about my dad?" she asked.

He'd neglected to ask because in fact, he didn't want to know. How could a dad leave his daughter with a drug addicted mom? Why didn't he try to get them some help?"

"I'm sorry for being rude, what's your dad's name, baby girl?"

"His name is Avery Ratman and he owns Ratman's Harmony House." Ratman couldn't believe his ears. That was his name. She did need him.

"It's a pleasure knowing his name. He's a lucky man to have a wonderful daughter like you. And guess what?"

"What?" she asked.

"He had a room in his house remodeled for his daughter." Shayla swung her arms around his neck. She didn't give him time to stand to embrace her back. She hugged him so tight. Sharon cried watching her daughter. She didn't realize how much Shayla longed for a father. Then both of them could tell that there was a deep concern on her mind. She let go of his neck, stood back, and looked at both of them.

"But I can't leave my Mama. She's just starting to get well," she said as tears formed in her eyes.

"Who ever said you had to leave your mama? She has her own room in my house. You both have your own rooms and you don't have to come in mine!" he joked.

Shayla began to cry, "Oh my, Mama, we are finally going home."

"We sure are, baby. God had a home waiting for us," Sharon said, crying as hard as Shayla.

"All right now; you two are going to make me cry and men don't cry unless they're alone," Ratman said.

"Yes, they do because you told me real men do cry," Shayla chastised him.

"We do, baby girl. We certainly do."

There was so much joy in the room. It felt like Christmas morning in a hospital room, in the middle of October. He'd given them the best gift ever, a place to call home and they'd given him a family. They laughed and talked a little more, and Shayla wanted to leave so she could go see her new room. Sharon wasn't due to leave the hospital for another week. God was working things out right before her very own eyes. She gave Him her heart, and He gave blessings.

JACQUELINE

Jacqueline felt like she never went to sleep. Denisia kicked her all night long. If this is what she had in store when she did have a child, she wasn't sure that she was ready.

She and Bradley had stayed up long after Hubert and Cheryl talking about life and where their lives were. Jacqueline was so happy to have him in her life. From the moment they met until now, she'd grown fonder of him by the minute. He had an awesome sense of humor and he wasn't ashamed to show his caring and gentle side.

She'd asked him to go with her to church and he'd agreed. Hubert gave him one of his suits to wear and she went to her old trunk and pulled out a dress for Denisia. Denisia was so amazed that Jacqueline had clothes that even fit her. They all dressed for service and met at the table for Sunday breakfast. This was going to be each of their last night at the ranch and things would go back to almost normal.

Jacqueline had thought about putting her house on the market and buying a home for her and Geraldine. Now for reasons right before her, she was beginning to rethink the move.

Even though Raphiel's murder happened at the house, there still was a sweet presence there. She thought she'd be afraid there but she wasn't at all. Bradley convinced her that the devil had no authority over her or her home. He'd told her that she should move only if she thought it would hinder her from moving forward. Or forever link her to Raphiel's death.

She decided to pray about it in morning worship and hoped God would give her an answer.

YOLANDA

Yolanda and Johnny got dressed for worship service. She could hardly wait until church was over, so she could get on that airplane. After she finished putting on her makeup, she came downstairs where Johnny was.

"How did you sleep Yolanda?"

"I slept well, Johnny, thank you. I went to sleep dreaming about our trip."

"Me too. Are you ready to go?"

"Yeah, let me do one thing."

"What's that?"

"I need to get my sword."

"Oh, your Word?"

"Yes, my Bible, and I'm ready now."

"Let's go. I've already packed our bags in the car. You can tell Jacqueline about our trip at church this morning."

"I didn't know you went to church with Jacqueline."

"All my life; I grew up there and so did she."

"This is going to be nice. I finally go to church and I'll be with the person who's been asking me to go for years. I do believe that God has a sense of humor."

"I know he does," Johnny said as he closed and locked the front door. He couldn't help but give her a kiss after he put her in the car. She was beautiful and she was the gift that God had given to him.

RAPHIEL'S AUNT

Geraldine woke up and put on her clothes. She needed to hear a word from the Lord. Her spirits were still kind of down but she wanted and needed to shake back.

The Lord had called Raphiel home and that was that. Doesn't matter how he went, it was his time. "Man didn't give him life and man couldn't take his life away."

She mumbled. It was time and God had things in control. She grabbed her bible off the coffee table and out of it fell a letter. She picked it up and it read….

Dear Aunt, Mom, Friend

I've done something horrible but I've asked God to forgive me. Aunt Geraldine you've been a mother to me and although I hate to leave you, I have to go. I need to go away to get my mind right. I've asked Jacqueline to forgive me and I pray she will. You've always told me to do what was right, but I let my ego get in the way.

You said that there is a way that seems right to man but it would lead to destruction and I'm there. I'm in the middle of my mess. One thing I know is that God is a forgiving God and he will receive me as His child.

I love you so much and I've deposited five hundred thousand dollars in your account. Take care of yourself until I get back and please take care of Jacque-

line. She'll need you no matter what. Even if she decides to be with someone else, I want you to stick with her because she loves you like a mother. Pray for me but please allow me to go on this journey in your heart.

Love Always,

Raphiel

Geraldine couldn't believe it. It was almost like he knew he was dying. He'd set everything in order before he left. Although she cried, her tears weren't because she was sad. She was crying tears of complete total joy. Her boy was saved and now he was resting in the bosom of Jesus. The money didn't matter because he'd never allowed her to spend her own money. She had over a million dollars saved and now this was more added to what she already had.

Now she had to grab her checkbook because she had to pay her tithes on this money. God was too good to her for her not to give Him what was His.

SHAYLA

Avery Ratman and Shayla dressed for church. He'd taken her to one of those teen stores to buy her some outfits. To his surprise, she was a very conservative dresser. She picked things that made her look like a young lady and he couldn't have been any more proud of her.

When she'd finished dressing and fixing up her hair, she met him downstairs. He never thought he'd feel this way, but when she came down the stairs, he felt like she was his very own seed. The first thing he was going to do was ask Sharon to get her last name changed to Ratman.

She deserved to have her father's name and so much more.

Hattie, Clarence, Corey, and Terry were in the car and on their way to church. Mrs. Vance called and invited them to her church and they'd decided that church would be good. Hattie wanted a new way of life for her boys. She'd lost T J to the streets and the devil and he was a lie if he thought he was going to get the others.

She was willing to do whatever she had to, to fight for their lives. As she looked at the three young men, she couldn't help but think of how blessed she was.

God had placed in her hands three kings and it was up to her to do right by them.

Sharon had the radio Avery brought her tuned in to KOKA. She was ready to hear the word from Morning Star Ministries. Avery had already set the dial where it needed to be and at nine, all she had to do was have a nurse to turn it on. It was almost nine so she called the nurse. They were already given instructions by Avery so she knew exactly why Sharon was calling. She went in and turned on Sharon's radio and told her to enjoy the service.

THE MESSAGE

"Praise the Lord Saints of God."

"Praise the Lord!" the crowd shouted back.

"Look at your neighbor and tell them, There is a word from the Lord."

"Turn in your word to Luke the fifth chapter and we're going to deal with the first through the twentieth verses." After the congregation stood and read in unison, Pastor Hunt asked everyone to take a seat.

"My subject today is: You're Not Too Far Gone. Touch your neighbor and tell them, 'Neighbor, you're not too far gone.'"

"As you see, this man was in a conditional state. Not only did he have an unclean spirit, but he'd had some adverse circumstances. And even some situations to happen with the people around him. Have you ever been in a situation where people saw that you needed a fix? They tried to fix you their way but it didn't work. See, that's why when the people bound this man, he always broke free. Folks can't fix your problems for you. No matter how hard it is for them to see in the state of needing fixing, they can't fix you. Can I get an amen?"

And the people shouted, "Amen!"

"Notice how when this man saw Jesus, he ran and worshiped Him. See, this shows that when folks need fixing they'll often run to Jesus.

Not because they know they have a problem, but because the folks have said they have a problem. How many of you know that people can't get help unless they want help? What I need the saints to know is that the prayers of the righteous availeth much. No matter how long it takes for them to recognize that they need fixing, you can't badger them. Your only job is to keep on praying for them. See, God wants you to know that His people are not too far gone, that He can't bring them back to Him. You do what you're supposed to do. Not judge them. Not push them into a fix. But pray for them. Can I get an amen?"

And the people shouted, "Amen!"

"Then look at how the demons in the man begged God not to torment him. Sounds familiar. As soon as they get out there too far and something happens, they start asking God not to kill them. See God has a way of getting folks to a place where the demons in them will abandon them. When God comes on the scene, addiction, fornication, lying, back biting, and adultery has to go. Sin can't dwell where God is. See, my friends, you are never too far gone where God can't come in.

"Then when Jesus comes in, He will create in you a clean heart and renew a right spirit within you. Anybody know that Jesus will clean you up? He will send the spirits that have been tormenting you, straight to hell. Spirits make you depressed, oppressed, and stressed, but God will cast them out. God is a good God. Don't ever think your situation has you so captive that God can't free you. He, whom the Son has set free, is free indeed."

"Hallelujah!" the congregation shouted.

"All you have to do is believe that there's nothing too hard for God. What seems impossible to man is possible for God. Remember Saints that God answers prayers. No matter how long it takes, God's timing is perfect timing."

Sharon sat in her bed listening to the message. Her eyes filled with tears. So many people had tried to get her to stop taking drugs. Yet, nothing stopped her until she had an encounter with Jesus herself. She knew at this moment more than ever that she was free. Free from the drugs, free from causing pain to her child, free from living in shelters. She was free and free indeed.

❦

Yolanda couldn't help but cry. As she sat there, Johnny held her in his arms. He knew that she was rejoicing for where God had her now. She was a changed person. She was like the demon possessed man. So many times Jacqueline tried to help her out, but she didn't want to come out. Now, she was out and she'd never go back again. Life had so much more to offer her and she wanted all God had in store for her.

❦

Some people were standing all over the room, clapping and praising God.

"Has God brought anybody out? Stand on your feet and give God the praise. He knows what you've gone through. He allowed you to go through so that when you came out, you could go and tell somebody what great things He's done for you. Not only that, He wants you to tell others of His compassion. God is compassionate. We have to have compassion on people because they're never too far gone. God can do exceedingly and abundantly above all we can ask, think, or feel according to the power that works in us. Don't you know that prayer is power? That's why it's imperative that we pray for one another. Pray them out. Pray them through. Come on, somebody give God some true worship. Come on, somebody praise the name of the Lord."

JACQUELINE & FRIENDS

Bradley didn't think any other pastor could preach as hard as Pastor Roderick Prince Strong. But now, he'd found one. This guy preached the word. It was a word of healing and compassion. If you never had compassion for anyone before, it made you want to have compassion like Jesus.

He sat there beside Jacqueline thinking how she'd had compassion on Yolanda. To see Yolanda over there on the other side praising God was awesome. Then he was even more moved when Jacqueline started singing. "I need you, you need me, we're all a part of God's body…"

It was his favorite song from Hezekiah Walker and he joined in. Before the song had finished, people were up hugging each other. People that Bradley had never seen before came up to hug him. Then Jacqueline stood beside him with her arm holding his waist. When he looked down into her eyes, she whispered, "Thank you for being my friend. I need you to survive." He kissed her on her forehead and said, "Ditto."

After service was over, everyone was so full of love. The atmosphere was still filled with kisses and hugs. As Yolanda found her way to her friend she was so grateful. Gratefulness was penetrating all in her heart and mind.

"Jacqueline, I want to thank you for not giving up on me. I guess you knew that I was not too far gone for God to come in and change me."

"Girl, I knew that you were my friend and I loved you."

"Well, Johnny is surprising me with a getaway. We are on our way to the airport. I didn't want to leave without telling you thanks."

"You are so welcome. Look, enjoy yourself. Forget about everything and everyone except Johnny and have fun."

"I'll try. I love you, Jacqueline."

"You know that I love you too, friend." And they hugged one another.

Geraldine walked over to where the two ladies were and waited on them to finish hugging. Then she hugged Yolanda and Yolanda met back up with Johnny who was telling Hubert about their trip.

"Jacqueline, sweetheart, I have something to tell you."

"Hey, Aunt Geraldine, how are you?"

"I'm fine, baby. Look, I know how you may be feeling about the house, so I am going to buy you another house."

"No Aunt Geraldine, you are not going to buy me a house but I am going to buy us a house."

"I have money, Jacqueline. Raphiel left me some money and you know he never let me spend any of my checks."

"I know all about the money he left you. It's for you to go on trips with me and shop until you drop. I am going to sell the house but I promise we will have a new house in a couple of weeks. In the meantime, we are going to stay at the ranch. Dad told me that he didn't mind. I know that in order for me to move on, I have to sell the house."

"Well, I understand. I see Bradley and Denisia came to church with you. I like him, Jacqueline, and he likes you too. You make sure he knows I am a part of you all's family and I ain't going nowhere."

Jacqueline looked as if she missed something then said, "We don't have a family, Auntie."

Aunt Geraldine laughed. "You will and I want to be a part of it."

"You'll always be with me until the Lord takes one of us home. I love you, Geraldine, and in case you didn't know, you are retired."

She giggled. "You mean I can't go to work anymore?"

"No, ma'am, you said that you are going to help me with my children so I'm going to be getting you ready to become a grandma one day. Grandma's don't work, they shop." And they laughed as they hugged each other.

"Mrs. Vance, Mrs. Vance."

Jacqueline turned around to see who was calling her.

"Hello, you two. I'm so glad to see the both of you." Clarence and Shayla were hand in hand as they came to greet Jacqueline.

"Mrs. Vance, you always said that I was not too far gone. And the preacher said the same thing."

Jacqueline touched Shayla's arm. "He did, Shayla."

Clarence chimed in with pure excitement. "We have something to tell you."

Jacqueline looked at them both and puckered her lips. "What have the two of you cooked up?"

They snickered and poked one another. "We are brother and sister. Shayla is my real sister."

Jacqueline put her hands on her hips. "Well, I'll be. That explains why the both of you are so stubborn." She laughed.

Shayla shrugged her shoulders. "I guess so."

Clarence grabbed his sister by the hand then said, "Mrs. Vance, thank you for everything."

Jacqueline pulled them both in for a hug. She released them and held both of their chins. "No, I want to thank the both of you. You two are mine and I am looking forward to seeing you do big things with your lives."

"Yes, ma'am," they said together in unison.

Jacqueline pointed at her wrist. "I love you all and I will see you both in class this week and on time."

"Yes, ma'am." They snickered and walked away the same way they came to her—hand in hand.

Bradley smiled at her. "Okay, Ms. Famous. Can I get you to come on so I can take my two favorite ladies somewhere?"

"You can, Mister." And Bradley caught Jacqueline by one hand and Denisia with the other and led them to the car.

"You know you're not too far gone for God to do a new thing in your life."

"So you don't say. What do you suppose He'll do next?"

"He'll give you a husband and a ready-made child."

"Whenever he does that, I'm sure I'll be able to handle it."

EPILOGUE

J acqueline and Yolanda stood in the church's bridal dressing
room alone. The other girls in the wedding party were in the
room adjacent to theirs. Jacqueline had planned it this way to
give the two of them some much needed time.

"Girl, would you come on here with your plump self and get into
this dress?"

Yolanda frowned. "I don't know if I can fit it."

"You better fit it. This is my wedding day and you and that big belly
of yours is going to get in this dress if I have to force you." Jacqueline
said as she struggled to zip the dress on Yolanda.

"You need to put on your wedding gown while you're worried about
me," Yolanda fussed.

Jacqueline laughed at Yolanda fussing as usual. The pregnancy had
made her even more of a drama queen. "I am. I'm trying to make sure
that you're ready. You know you can't put your shoes on."

Yolanda rolled her eyes. "So. Stop reminding me how big my belly is.
In one more month, I'll be bringing this little one to your doorstep,"
Yolanda said as she rubbed her belly.

"Okay, I guess I can go put my things on. I know Bradley is waiting
for his beautiful wife to come down the aisle."

"He sure is," Jacqueline blushed.

"I hate that you and Johnny eloped. You could have done it here so we all could have been a part," Jacqueline said, scolding her friend.

"We thought that with the baby and all, we'd like to be married. He didn't want the baby to come here without having his last name. I was happy that he was willing to marry me carrying another man's baby."

"When God does it, nothing matters."

"Raphiel is gone and this baby is going to need a daddy and Johnny knows that."

"He's such a good man, Jacqueline. I don't know what I would have done raising this child all by myself."

"You know that Geraldine would have helped you. She is so excited that you are pregnant. We all are and I know Raphiel would have been happy."

"I often wonder what God was thinking about. It almost seems like a soap opera. I sleep with my friend's husband, he gets murdered, I'm pregnant with his child, and now married to another man."

"If that doesn't deserve the front page of a rag magazine," Jacqueline said.

"And all I can say is, 'God knows.' He knows exactly what He has done and it's all good," Yolanda said.

"It is and look at me. Who would have ever thought that I'd be getting married so soon. Eight months after Raphiel's death, I have a ready-made family. A husband who is so loving and kind; and a daughter who is so smart. And Yolanda, who would have ever thought Shayla and Clarence would be at and walking in my wedding."

"Girl, this lets me know that we are not too far in our own agendas that God can't install His plan right in the mix."

"You're right about that." Jacqueline said and the two ladies shared one last laugh before Jacqueline went to meet her KING.

SPECIAL THANKS

Hello Faithful Readers,

I just want to thank you and to those who have just discovered books by ME, thank you for taking the chance on a new-to-you author.

If you enjoyed NOT TOO FAR please take some time and leave a REVIEW!

Listen, you may be going through some things. Broken. Feeling like you are in the world all alone. But let me remind you that you are never alone. There is a SAVIOR who promised to never leave nor forsake you, and His name is Jesus. So today…not tomorrow, not next year, but TODAY, give HIM your life.

You can do this simply by saying this:

Father, come into my heart, and forgive me for all of my sins. I declare with my mouth Jesus is Lord, and I believe in my heart that God raised Jesus from the dead. And this day, I am saved.

If you read this and believe it, Congratulations and Welcome into the KINGDOM!

Now, to help you on your journey, I have more books that will guide you along the way.

CHECK out some books from the Keatchie Corner Series: PRAY INTENSE- the story of Ricky & Charlotte, POTENTIAL - the story of

Buddy & Candice, NEED- the story of Dominique & Erica, HEALED- the story of Cody & Jennifer, WEAK-the story of Miguel & Bianca, DREAM the story of Mya & Dalton, STRUGGLE- the story of Kevin & Tanya, GUILTY- the story of Ryan & Heaven, PLENTY- the story of Logan & Angel, and the first book in this series FOUND, the story of Gotrell & Paisley.

Here's also another awesome story of a power couple (Maddox & Gazelle) I know you'll love:

MR. COMPETITIVE

Want a FREE BOOK, join my mailing list and get MORE THAN DIAMONDS.

ABOUT THE AUTHOR

Danyelle Scroggins is the Pastor of New Vessels Ministries in Shreveport, Louisiana. She is the author of special books like Put It In Ink, Graced After The Pain, Evonta's Revenge, & Enduring Love. Danyelle is also a Chaplain at Ochsner LSU St. Mary in Shreveport. She's the wife of Pastor Reynard Scroggins and the mother of three young adults: Raiyawna, Dobrielle, and Dwight Jr. by birth; and two: Reynard II and Gabriel by marriage. She's privilege to be the grandmother of Emiya'rai Grace, RC III, & Maddox Rai.

Danyelle loves writing inspirational stories set in Louisiana, where she lives preaching, teaching, and enjoying writing by the window. Learn all about her here www.danyellescroggins.com.

Also find her on Facebook, Twitter, and Bookbub.

facebook.com/authordanyellescroggins

twitter.com/pastordanyelle

bookbub.com/profile/danyelle-scroggins

goodreads.com/danyellescroggins

ALSO BY DANYELLE SCROGGINS

Made in the USA
Columbia, SC
26 September 2024

43091799R00152